Olivia's Flight

LOVE AND VAMPIRES

RHIANNON FUTCH

Contents

Chapter One

OLIVIA

The ceiling needs refinished.

I need to get outside. Into the world. Somewhere I'm not stuck in a house staring at a ceiling so long I've cataloged its every flaw. This hiding is beyond ridiculous. Since I'm the one exploding, I'm not entirely certain who exactly I am hiding from. Realizing the sound of Nims licking the dish I set out for her has stopped, I sit up. The clock on the wall says it's time to go. Jumping out of bed, I run over to grab the bowl and stuff it into the drawer. It slides shut just as Duncan opens the door after a quick knock.

He stares at me a moment. "What are you doing?"

"Putting away my fucking delicates. Refresh my memory. When did I give you permission to track everything I do?"

He has the grace to look embarrassed, for all that we aren't able to blush. "It's time to go to Ailsa's for your lesson. Are you ready?"

"We'll be right down."

I wait for him to close the door before I grab the towel from behind me and give Nims face a thorough cleaning to get any of my blood that might be left on her. A bit of scented shea butter and she should pass all but the most intense of inspections.

I don't know what they would do if they found out that I was feeding her my blood. But I'll take that risk again and again until she is immune to the effects of the sun.

Moments later, we are traipsing down the stairs to the main floor entry, where Duncan and Callum wait for us. They are both smiling at me until Duncan notices Callum's smile. He scowls and opens the front door. "Move it, pretty boy."

Callum turns and bats his lashes at Duncan. "You think I'm pretty?"

Nims and I sail on past them and get in the car. I don't need any of Duncan's weird jealousy thing. Rubbing at the spot on my chest that seems to flair when something unpleasant happens, I arrange my legs to be on either side of Nims.

They get in the car and I hear the driver's door close just before we take off. The ride to Ailsa's is fast and monotonous. I've seen it twice a day since the explosion. Nothing changes. I think it is even the same car each time. It smells like the same car.

When we arrive, Duncan gets out first to check for other vampires. I really don't think they are going to send more vampires after the last set were turned into so much dust. Nims and I climb out next, Callum following. The witch at the counter takes one look at me and her lips press together. Rubbing at my chest as I walk over, I ask her, "Is Ailsa ready for me?"

She rolls her eyes and says, "Come along, princess. I hope you're grateful. No one else gets lessons from Ailsa."

Something in me snaps. I snarl at her. "Did you ever fucking stop to think that I didn't choose this? That maybe this isn't for me, but so I'm not a danger to anyone else? Or are you too wrapped up in jealousy to pull your head out of your ass and think logically?"

Nims is growling at the witch too. She has become very pale and backed against the far wall. Taking a deep breath and a long exhale, I say, "I'm sorry. Let's try to forget I said anything." Nims bulk presses against my leg and my hand drops to scratch her head. "Let's forget this and just take me to Ailsa. I'm sorry, I'm on edge and what you said hit me wrong. I hope you'll forgive me."

The witch leads me back as I rub at that spot on my chest again. It feels like something is trying to claw its way out of me.

Duncan

Fuck, is she going to explode? Are we about to have an incident? Will her emerging power cause our entire line to be wiped off the map? She's been rubbing her chest a lot lately. Is that how she's keeping herself in check? I can smell the blood and excitement from that fucking lunatic

Callum. Over there stabbing his tongue with his tooth while watching Olivia lose her temper. Does he not understand the danger here? That we could all die because she lost control?

The witch that gave her static seems to realize her error and shows Olivia and Nims to Ailsa's office. I'd give anything, including my life, to keep her safe, but I don't know how to keep her safe from herself. Snapping at a stranger, even if she deserved it, is out of character for her.

Callum's elbow hits my ribs. I glare at him as he says, "Calm down, for fuck's sake. She is learning, she's here to learn more. She didn't even heat the room up this time. She's doing great. You worry too much and trust her too little."

"I should be able to do more for her. Protect her better. Even from herself."

Callum waves a dismissive hand at me. "Let her be. You'll do her no favors by smothering her with your enormous ego."

"No one asked you. It's not like you have any room to talk as you snatched her away from everyone to your house where she was imprisoned and starved by your mother. As I recall, she was still half gone when you brought her back here, where she belongs."

Callum raises a brow. "Care to discuss this outside?"

My hands clench at my sides. "I'd love to, but we both know better. I need to go take care of some things. You'll stay here and wait for her? Let me know when she gets out? Think you can manage that much? Or should I send for someone that can follow directions?"

"Of course. I will message you the minute she informs me she is finished." He smiles, and I am not comforted by the smile. I need to get back here as soon as possible. Turning on my heel, I stride out of the witch's shop, determined to get back here before she finishes.

Chapter Two

Blair

Ailsa and I are waiting outside her home when Olivia, Nims, and the witch guiding them arrive. Olivia looks unhappy, and she's rubbing a spot on her chest. The moment she sees me, her face lights up. She runs over with Nims on her heels. Ailsa walks over to the witch and they speak briefly. She must have used magic to keep the conversation from being heard because not so much as a whisper of sound reaches me.

Olivia hugs me hard, and I can smell a combination of anger and anxiety on her. Nims leans into the both of us and Olivia lowers one arm to pat her. That explains why Ailsa is keeping the conversation private. The witch leaves, looking upset as Ailsa walks over with a smile. "Are we ready to get started?"

Olivia releases me and turns to say, "Yes. I'm ready. Let's get me in control of this magic that I shouldn't have to begin with."

Ailsa has an odd look on her face as she tells Olivia to

stand a few feet away from me and protect me however she can. Olivia's eyes round and Ailsa says, "Don't worry, I won't be shooting to kill. It won't even hurt much."

That's super comforting to me...

Ailsa fires her first shot and Olivia does something that causes it to change direction just before it hits me. Shot after shot, Ailsa fires at me and Olivia dissipates it or sends it another way. Sometimes she seems to have a little force field of sorts in front of me that the shots hit and are absorbed by. I am in awe of how well she is doing, even as she castigates herself for not having her power fully under control within a few weeks of it appearing.

Anyone else would give their right arm for the kind of control she is displaying right now. Why can't she see how well she is doing?

Olivia

I am dripping sweat by the time Ailsa calls for an end to the session. Blair walks over and says, "You did great. The way you talked, I was braced for impact at first. But you didn't let a single one hit me. I don't think most other magic users can do that within a few weeks of their power coming in, especially all at once, like yours did."

Ailsa walked over while Blair was talking, and she nods her agreement. "He's right. It is rare for anyone to have their full powers pop out of nowhere and be able to manage them the way you have." She looks away and sighs. "Your powers don't operate the same as witch powers do. It doesn't work quite the same. Now that I have a better idea of how they do work, I think we'll progress much faster."

"Well, if they aren't witch powers, what are they?"

"I am not sure exactly." She looks away. "I have some ideas, but I need to do some research first. I promise, if I figure it out, I will let you know immediately. No hiding it from you like you're a child or some shit."

"Thank you. That actually makes me feel a lot better about all this. Especially living with all these secretive damn vampires. It's ridiculous what they keep hidden."

Ailsa and Blair laugh. Ailsa says, "They love their secrets. The only vampires I've met that weren't neck deep in secrets hadn't been in vampire society much. Their sires had kept them sequestered from it. I've often wondered if it was a disservice to them just because of the shock to their way of thinking when they finally rejoined the world. But, you need to go eat something. Doing so much magic will deplete your resources if you don't eat often enough. You should have some blood with your lunch, too."

That spot in the middle of my chest is aching again. Rubbing at it, I tell her, "Yes. Maybe I can get clearance to have lunch out today." My lips twist as if I had eaten a lemon, even saying that. I hate this enforced isolation. I have plenty of people around me, but I'm not free to go as I please.

Ailsa laughs. "You should give yourself clearance. If they don't like it, you could always put one of your force fields around them."

"I like the idea. But won't they just be worse after?"

She shrugs, "Only if you let them. What are they going to do? You are your own person. These vampires, they want to help, but they are overbearing and rude about it. Maybe you'll be the one to convince them to act differently. Well, these vampires. It's a little much to expect that it would spread throughout the entirety of the vampire community. Now, give me a hug and go. You need food. You're looking pale, even for a vampire."

Chapter Three

Callum

Once Duncan leaves, I position myself against a section of wall near the door that is fairly empty. It also gives me a direct view of the door Olivia will come back through when her lessons are done. Pulling out my phone, I pass the time with silly games while I wait. No one pays me any mind beyond a casual glance at the stranger holding up the wall. The backroom door opens, and it's her. She looks a little pale, as if she were hungry. Nims is trotting right next to her, staying close enough to brush up against her. I think that is her tell. And how I can reliably know when Olivia is anxious about something. Blair follows her out and I am oddly relieved. The wolf has a good head on his shoulders and he truly cares about her.

If she is going to have multiple partners, he is a good choice for one. I watch as she spots me and she almost smiles. After looking around further, she asks, "Did Duncan leave?"

"Yes. He said he needed to go work on his attitude. I told him I would let him know when you finished." Smiling, I ask her, "Are you finished?"

She looks confused for a moment, but understanding dawns fast. Blair caught on instantly and he is grinning behind her. Olivia says, "No, I'm not finished. I would love to go to the bookstore and possibly find somewhere to eat? Not necessarily in that order?"

"Your wish is our command." I move to stand next to her and Nims, leaving Nims plenty of space to walk between us.

Blair is on her other side as we leave the building. He asks, "Should we take her to the place on the other side of the block from my mom's shop? With a stop in the shop to get Nims some treats, of course."

"I think that place will be great for a nice long lunch. And Nims must be ready for some treats."

Nims dances and gives a happy little howl, making Olivia laugh. Olivia says, "That sounds wonderful. Let's go." I watch as she rubs her chest again while we walk. Meeting Blair's eyes, I know he has been noticing it too. I wonder what it means.

Olivia

Walking in the sunlight with Nims, Blair, and Callum is amazing. I want to do this more. Blair's mother is the sweetest woman, and she was so happy to see Nims again.

She got down on her knees to hug my Nims. I can't remember feeling this much carefree joy in way too long. Even the ache in my breastbone is subsiding. Once Nims picked her treats, we left the store and walked around to the other side of the block. Callum pointed the windows out to me first. They are a work of magical art. The restaurant is called A Taste of Spring and the windows are full of flower petals that are continually rearranging themselves into floral arrangements and pictures. It is breathtaking. If I wasn't so hungry I would stay to watch them for a time. But I am hungry. I feel like my belly is eating itself.

The restaurant is really nice without being super upscale on the inside. The chairs look comfortable and the tables are big. Plenty of space to enjoy food and company. A human shaped creature with flowers sprouting from them in various places comes to greet us. Blair greets them with a smile and a hug, which they return.

He tells them, "These are my friends, Olivia, Nims, and Callum. Everyone, this is Ess. None of us are equipped to say their name, and that is the one they prefer from those that need an alternative."

Ess greets each of us with a handshake or, in Nims case, a pat. "Come, I will take you all to one of the private rooms. Vampires love private rooms."

I laugh as we follow them. Callum looks chagrined. The pained smile is kind of cute on him. If only... but no. The private room is spacious and more upscale than the front room appeared. I would have liked to eat out there and get to people watch. Maybe I can get Blair to come back with me sometime soon? Another little escape from Roman and

Duncan's fierce overprotection would do great things for my attitude, at least. If not for my supposed safety. Ess takes our drink orders, producing menus from somewhere. They leave for the drinks while we study the menus. I have eaten out anywhere only a little, so I ask Blair, "What do you suggest?"

He says, "The Scotch pies are great here and they feel a bit like being wrapped in a cozy blanket in front of a fire at home. That might be nice for you right now."

"That sounds perfect. Scotch pie it is. I don't care if it's stuffed with haggis."

Blair and Callum both laugh. Blair says, "No haggis in the pie. I know the Americans are certain it's a terrible dish, but it is really very good. I'm ordering some myself. I could let you try a bite if you decide you are interested."

"Ok, I will. I'll try two new things today."

Callum offers, "I am getting the cock-a-leekie soup. If you want to try something that feels like a warm hug in all the best ways, you are welcome to sample it."

I am delighted with this. They are both being so generous and caring. Plus, offering to share food. I worry about getting too attached to Callum. He said that I was nothing, but maybe... maybe it was just to Diane. Maybe he was trying to protect me from her. Ess returns with our drinks and takes our orders. They seem approving of our choices and I am glad I ordered the Scotch pie. The two men entertain me with stories of escapades past. Blair starts with a tale of stealing all the eggs from his mother's coop and hiding them throughout the yard and the house. His mother was very mad about the ones she didn't find till weeks later. Apparently, even wolf senses can be fooled with scents. Callum tells tales of court intrigue as a new vampire long ago, before things were so set in stone.

Ess brings us our food and we dig in. Nims is happily feasting on tasty chunks of meat chopped into bite-size pieces arranged into a stack on her plate. Well, bite sized for her. My Scotch pie is amazing. The crust is perfection and Blair was right; it feels like being wrapped in a warm blanket in front of a fire. Callum spoons a bit of his soup and offers me first taste. I allow him to feed me and I am transported into bliss. It is the best chicken soup I have ever had, and it really feels like a warm hug from a mother that cares.

Blair waits till I am finished with the warm hug of the soup and asks, "Do you still want to try the haggis?"

"I do. Yes, please."

He grins, "Here you go." He brings a forkful of haggis over and stops an inch away from my mouth, letting me lean in to take the bite. It smells great. It tastes like a gamey sort of sausage. I see why he likes it so much. From what I know, wolves prefer wild meat to domesticated.

"I think I could like that. It tastes much better than I have been led to believe."

Blair grins and nods, saying, "I'm glad you like it."

We carry on eating and talking. Nims even offers her two cents a few times. My chest isn't aching right now. I want more days like this. More days of good food, conversation, and my Nims beside me. More bliss.

It all comes crashing to a stop when Duncan storms in. "What are you doing here? This was not part of the plan for today."

I speak up. "Duncan, I needed to eat after my session. Today was grueling. Come on and sit down. Eat with us.

We're in a private room. No one is going to see us from the street. It's fine. Don't spoil it, please?"

Duncan argues, "They could just follow the scent and trail you all left like a giant flag marking your location for anyone trying to find you."

I can feel the anger building again. My chest hurts, and I hate him a little for bringing the pain back. "I'm not leaving until I have finished eating. Will you sit and join us or wait outside?"

Duncan nods, his face grim, and Ess sets a chair down for him. They are amazing. The chair was just suddenly in their hands. Duncan sits and tells Ess his order. They leave and return quickly with his drink. Ess brings him a steak and potatoes meal not long after that. Once they leave, Duncan says, "Callum, why didn't you let me know she was finished immediately? I could have dropped what I was doing and come to escort you all home. And Blair, you are usually so level-headed and watching for her safety. What happened to that?"

It's only when Nims growls that I realize I have a hand on her and the other on my chest. It hurts so much. The pain is sharp, like being stabbed with long needles over and over again. But all I can think about is how he is ruining my meal with his shit attitude. I guess Nims is picking up on my emotions. She has always been my most fierce protector.

All three men freeze, their eyes locked on us. Duncan leans back and says, "I'm sorry. I wasn't thinking. I'm concerned about your safety. I was probably over-reacting. I'm just worried for you."

I am so sick of their stifling worry and I snarl at him,

"You are smothering me. I am not hiding anymore. I've had—"

Ess walks in and clears their throat, "Ma'am, our cooling spell is working overtime to maintain the temperature in here. If he can't behave, we'll put him out, but could you please not heat the building like this?"

I am stunned and embarrassed. Clamping down on my powers, I say, "I am so sorry. I will keep them under wraps. I think he will behave now. There is no need to remove him."

Ess eyes him suspiciously, "Are you sure? It's no trouble and you were fine until his arrival."

I laugh and the tension in the room eases. "I appreciate that, but no. He will behave or I will leave."

Ess leaves with one last scathing glance at Duncan. Putting my head in my hands, I mumble, "I don't understand why you all keep me around. You can't even have a heated discussion without me trying to burn the place down."

They all reassure me that the entire incident was Duncan's fault, even if my reaction wasn't what I wanted. Then Callum points out that Nims and my eyes were glowing red.

Duncan asks, "Do we really need to point that out now?"

Callum presses his tongue into that tooth before answering. The scent of his blood tinges the air momentarily. He says, "I don't believe in hiding things or holding them back because it might upset her. I know she's an adult. Did you not notice?"

Duncan snarls something, but Blair cuts him off. "I'll have Ess toss you out if you start your shit again. And I'll follow you out to beat some fucking sense into you. Don't try me. She was at ease and happy before you came in. She wasn't even rubbing that spot on her chest. "

Duncan narrows his eyes at them but quiets as his eyes come to rest on me, still rubbing at my chest. He swallows whatever he wanted to say and nods. We all finish our food but the happy mood is ruined.

Chapter Four

I never thought I would be sneaking out of a house again once I left my parents' place, but I need to talk to Ailsa. I'm not being unsafe exactly, just not letting all the vampires know my business. Nims and I are near the wall at the far end of the garden. It isn't unusual for us to come out here. We should have at least ten minutes before anyone "wanders out" to check on us.

"All right, I'm going to boost you up to the top of the wall. You lay down like you are part of the wall. We can both jump down after we know we won't be landing on anyone."

Nims nods, and she cooperates when I pick her up and lift her onto the wall. She could have sailed over it, but not being able to see the other side makes me nervous. Once she is pressed as flat as she can against the top of the wall, I jump up to grab the wall and pull myself up. After a making sure no one will be under us, we jump down and start walking for the corner that I told Blair to meet us at.

Someone steps out of the bushes to my left and I swing before I check who it is, my fist connecting with a face. The man grabs my wrist; I look at his face. Fuck. "Are you going to force us to go back?"

Callum grins, his lips still bloody, "No. I'm not here to enforce the rules, only to make sure you and Nims are safe. Where are we going?"

"We? I didn't plan to take anyone except Blair."

"I'm glad you are thinking about your safety. Why Blair?"

"Because he isn't a shady fucking vampire that keeps things from me."

Callum puts a hand over his heart. "You wound me with your accuracy. I'll make you a deal. Let me go with you on any escapades you go on without the rest of the vampires and I'll answer any question you ask of me, truthfully."

Thinking about his proposition, I remember all the times that the rest of them told me something, but it was so convoluted that I didn't realize until much later what they were actually saying. "In plain language? No talking in circles or vague non-answers?"

He nods. "Plain language and no subterfuge. Promise."

"Is there a time limit?"

He smiles. "You've been around too many vampires. No. For you and Nims, no time limit. Ask your questions at any time and I will answer to the best of my knowledge and ability, barring secrets that are not my own to tell. Anything outside of that is fair game."

"Ok. That's fair. Very well. I accept your deal. Now let's go. Blair has been waiting long enough."

The walk to the corner is short, and Blair's only

reaction to Callum's presence is an eyebrow raise. I shrug. "He caught us sneaking out."

Blair smiles, saying, "And you came along rather than rat her out? Good. I approve. Though it is very un-vampire-like of you."

Callum laughs. Shaking his head, he says, "Just what I've always longed for, wolf approval."

Rolling my eyes, I tell them, "Guys, flirt later. I have things to do and I need to get to the magic sector to do them."

Blair says, "My van is over here." He leads us down the block to where he has it parked. As he opens the door for me, he says, "I was at work and it was faster to bring the van than to go home and get my car. Mom was fine with it. She said that you should come by the shop. "

Nims barks her agreement, and I let her jump in before me. She is quickly in the back of the van and I get into the passenger seat. Blair opens the side door for Callum, who says, "Thank you, much appreciated. Is this part of the flirting later?"

Blair grins at him. "You'll know it if I flirt with you, vampire." He shuts the door behind Callum and walks around to get in the van. The drive is short and no one even looks twice at the pet shop delivery van. It is the perfect way to travel. We have a little walk to get to Ailsa's shop when we get there. Parking is always at a premium in this country.

The witch at the counter is the same one that was mean to me last time. She grimaces as I walk in. I take a breath, rubbing at the spot in my chest that just about always hurts now, and ask, "Is Ailsa available to talk to me?"

The witch says, "One moment, please." Her eyes get

cloudy for a bit and when they clear, she says, "You may go back, and your companions can go with you."

"Thank you."

She nods and goes back to her duties as we move to the end of the counter and the small pass thru. The door opens as we get to it, allowing us to pass through before it closes behind us. The door down the hall is open once again. This time when I walk in Nims and I are in her living area. Blair and Callum are right behind us, though unusually quiet.

Ailsa greets us and bids us to sit. Then she asks, "What is troubling you? I don't think you would be here if something wasn't concerning you deeply."

She's watching me intently, her eyes focused on the hand rubbing at the tender spot in the center of my chest. "I, well, I had another incident with heating a room at the restaurant down the street. But more than that, it feels like something is trying to claw its way out of my chest."

Ailsa's eyes widen. "It can't be! He was defeated. She sent him to hell herself! There haven't been any more in so long." She jumps out of her chair and dashes through the house. Nims and I look at each other, then we jump up and follow her. I can hear Blair and Callum following us as we enter what looks like a home library. Ailsa is flipping pages in a large book like a life depends on it and I have the sinking feeling that the life is mine. When she stops on a page, I lean forward a bit to read as well.

- Lilith -

Goddess and Mother of Demons. Lured into a garden created by the God of men, who intended her to be the mate for his creation. She broke out of the garden prison when the man attempted to subjugate her. The God of men sent his warriors, called angels, after her. She fought many, loved a few. Those unions infuriated the God of men and he cursed any child produced from those unions. Thus, all her children became demons. The God of men set his warriors to slaughter her children. Because they were half his line, he sentenced them to hell upon their deaths. They promptly started possessing his followers and creating chaos.

One of her demon children escaped the hunts, only later to be sent to hell by Lilith herself for the crime of causing the humans to hunt the magical society. His part in the Inquisition, the Witch Trials, and various other church led massacres were crucial in that they would not have happened without his interference.

His most heinous crimes were against the women he impregnated while pretending to be a god, and the children of those unions that he had put to death.

Note: A very few of those children escaped before adulthood and the sacrifice they were created to be. Of those few, nearly all died when the demon side of them emerged.

Every one of his children complained of pain in the chest. This is the only symptom each had in common. Their emerging abilities were never fully catalogued as they died from fear when the demon side emerged.

Ailsa closes the book and carries it to a chair where she sits heavily. Sighing, she says, "I suppose it was naïve of us to think he would stay in hell where she put him. Roman told me about your parents. But I never, I had all but forgotten about this. It was such a dark time. I think we were all glad to put it behind us."

Nims is pressed hard against my leg, my hand resting on her head. "I don't know if I am understanding. What does that entry mean?"

Ailsa looks me in the eye as she tells me, "If I am right, it means that your mother copulated with Lilith's son to become pregnant with you in exchange for a life of luxury. Which means you are part demon, a daughter of Ahriman. But also granddaughter of Lilith. Your powers are emerging and, with them, your demon side. I cannot be certain of the timeline, but your demonic side will emerge soon and integrate with you."

My breath catches as I look down at my Nims, "Will it kill me? When it emerges?"

"No. It isn't terribly pleasant, but it doesn't actually do any damage. Your mind is still your own. It is, in a literal sense, just an emergence of power as far as we know. Though few have ever lived through it. That was more on account of fear than anything." She sighs and shakes her head. "This also means that you all will need to be in on a little secret. I can't challenge you, train you in the way that you need if I maintain the facade during our sessions. We would all greatly prefer that you not let anyone know that we witches don't age anymore than you all do."

As she speaks, the air surrounding her seems to get fuzzy and when it clears, holy shit. Ailsa looks like the age I was when I was turned. Her white hair is now long and dark in a braid down her back. The wrinkles on her face are gone, her body shape remains the same, as do her eyes.

"How long have you had to keep that illusion up when you're in public?"

She smiles ruefully. "A few decades or more. I don't go outside the magic sector and the people inside it are slower to become suspicious of the years not passing."

Blair laughs. Ailsa looks at him with raised brows. He sobers and says, "You probably should make sure that Roman doesn't see you like that. With the way sparks fly between the two of you... if he realizes how much like him you are, there will be nothing stopping him from getting closer to you."

Ailsa's eyes go round and a little of the color drains from her face. "Luckily, he isn't invited to Olivia's lessons, and I will not be out in public without my elderly appearance."

Callum asks, "Will the emergence be explosive as well? And, at some point, perhaps we should address that the dog's eyes now glow in tandem with Olivia's?"

Ailsa looks at me, "Is this true?"

Shrugging, I say, "I don't know? I didn't know my eyes were glowing. He isn't a liar, so I have to assume that they were."

Callum says, "It happened at dinner. When Duncan was acting a fool after your last lesson. You had a hand on Nims like you always do and as the temperature in the restaurant rose, your eyes were red and glowing, so were Nims."

Ailsa stands and walks over to us. She tells me, "Kneel down here with Nims and I. I need to touch you both." I do as she said, and she places a hand on my head and the other on Nims head. Her eyes droop and close. I can feel a whisper of coolness spread through me. Her eyes fly open. "There is a channel open between the two of you. What happens to one also happens to the other. Nims wasn't born a demon, but her connection to you is giving her demon power, regardless."

Blair asks the one question on my mind, "Will that hurt Nims? Is she going to experience the same symptoms?"

Ailsa stands, shaking her head no. "She will only get the benefit and the immunity from her power. Olivia, you no longer need to worry that you will hurt Nims with your power. However, it means we need to figure out how to train her. If she is going to have this power, Nims will have to know how and when to use it. No one needs a dog, even a smart one, running around with untrained abilities."

Duncan

"The reports aren't good."

Roman snorts, "Tell me something I don't know."

Looking back at the reports, I say, "The number of Italian vampires in the city doubled overnight."

Roman stands and crosses the room to stare out the window. His silence is only broken when he says, "Call everyone home. Effective immediately. The entire family. We are bracing for war, and we'll need everyone."

Niall nods, "What about those that are on diplomatic missions?"

Roman shrugs, "We can't be certain which families are

not tainted by the church that is after Olivia. They didn't get to Callum's mother after Olivia arrived. She was already working with them. We don't know who can be trusted. Even within the family, those that will be returning, some haven't been home in decades. We'll need to monitor everyone for a time."

Shit. He's right. We are going to have our people working extra just to verify everyone as they come home. Maybe I can have them start checking into what they have been doing before they come home? That might speed the process and make the amount of extra hours needed smaller.

Roman is telling us he is expecting there will be a large attack soon, between the numbers of Italian vampires flocking to the area and the church members doing the same. Then he looks at me, "Duncan, I need you to go to Ailsa's and make sure that Olivia is with you any time she is outside this house. Callum and Blair are good, but they aren't my enforcer and she is like the daughter I never had. I want her safe. And I want you to stop inciting her. If my house gets burnt to the ground because you are pissing her off, I'll kick your ass myself."

"It's not like I do it intentionally."

Niall turns his face away to hide a smile I can still see as Roman says, "You also don't intentionally fix the problem, either. You can fix the problem and it doesn't take much. She isn't asking you to climb Everest. But I am. If that is what you need to do, then you better climb fucking Everest."

Niall has turned fully away and his shoulders are shaking. Fucker. "I will work on it. I just, I worry about her.

I mean fuck, she just snuck out. It's like she has no concept of the danger she is in."

"She would if you told her." Roman crossed his arms over his chest as he said that, then continues, "Olivia is not a delicate flower. She is a little demon that hasn't fully realized how dangerous she is. Duncan, she is a vampire that can set shit on fire with magic and she has a dog that is equally powerful who lives to be by her side. If she ever figures out how powerful she is, they will turn our world upside down. If my guess is right, turning our world upside down is exactly what the witches expect from her. The worst danger she is in comes from not knowing. I've tried waiting for you to treat her like an equal. Your time is up. She could have walked out the front door with guards if she had known. You knew, but you wanted her closeted to keep her safe the way you want. That ends today. You tell her or I will as soon as she returns."

"Very well. I'm off to see her now. Niall, you don't need my help to call everyone back, correct? Once you are finished laughing, that is. I will work on starting the process to check into all the family members' doings when I return. I think we will be able to get at least half of them done before people trickle in. Except for the ones that drop everything and hop on a plane immediately. Keep me posted on travel plans as well, Niall?"

Niall finally turns to face me, his face suitably composed, and says, "Absolutely." Looking to Roman, he says, "If that is all, I'll start now?"

Roman waves him off. He closes the door behind him as he leaves and Roman gives me a dark look. "Our world is going to change and we must be at the forefront of the changes. All of us will have to be on board or our family will be left behind. We have the chance to rise in the ranks and I plan to make sure we do. The only question that remains is, will you be able to keep up?"

"I will. Now, if you'll excuse me..." He waves me away and turns back to stare out the window as I leave.

Chapter Five

Olivia

My chest hurts still as I come out of the back room and into the shop proper. Nims is at my side as always, Blair and Callum walking ahead of me. I know they would comfort me by saying it was to open doors or something, but I know better. They are going first in case there are more vampires waiting to attack me.

Fortunately, the only vampire waiting is Duncan. He frowns when he sees Callum and Blair. It hurts a little that his frown deepens when he sees me. Then he says, "We need to get you home. Now. It isn't safe for you to be wandering the streets with just a vampire and a wolf."

It feels as though time slows to the pace of a snail when his words hit me. I watch Blair and Callum turn to look back at me, a question in their eyes. I can feel a pulsing anger raging through my veins alongside the fear. Fear that he will force me to be locked up in some house forever just because these people want to hurt me and he wants to do things the vampire way.

Something in me snaps at the idea of being locked up in that house for another minute, and I say, "No."

Time slams back to normal speed as Blair smiles and Callum smirks as he mouths, "Good girl."

A frisson of desire runs through me from out of nowhere and I am thinking I might have a little kink in me somewhere.

Duncan's eyes narrow. "Yes, you are. It isn't safe for you out here."

"Duncan, who do you think you are talking to? You don't own me. You've been too long in your vampire hierarchy and it shows. Your ideas about how you are going to treat me are insane. Fuck off. I just got news about me and I need to process it. I want food while I do the processing. I'm going to go right down the street to A Taste of Spring and I'm going to have a private room and we are going to eat, drink, and relax. You may come with us if you are that concerned for my welfare, but you better act right, or it will be the last time you get anywhere near me."

The witch's shop is still and silent. Blair and Callum are facing Duncan now. Their stances shifted slightly. I think they mean to stop Duncan if he tries to get to me. I love that. I don't think anyone has ever tried to protect me like that, certainly no man. Duncan eyes them and me before sighing and he says, "Look, I really just want to keep you safe. The number of Italian vampires here has more than doubled. The church cult people? Also flooding the city. I am afraid for you."

"I will burn them to ashes before I let them take me. To ashes. And I'm almost certain that I can direct the flames at individuals now. I will not be hiding."

Duncan nods, saying, "I see your point and while that is fine inside the magical sector, it isn't super practical outside of it."

"It is if they seem to spontaneously self combust. Now, I am going to eat. I am angry, hungry, and the sharp edge of hangry is creeping in. Come along or get out of the way, but I am going to leave now."

Blair

For a moment, I thought we were going to watch Duncan die. I had serious doubts about his intelligence and sense of self-preservation. Olivia's and Nims' eyes were glowing red again and I don't know if she was fully in control the whole time. We all scan the area around us as we walk to A Taste of Spring.

We get in the restaurant and Olivia steps forward and speaks to the hostess before any of us can. "Hi, would it be possible for us to have a private room?"

The hostess checks her chart and smiles up at Olivia. "Yes, we have two available. How many?"

"Five, thank you so much."

The hostess gathers up menus and utensils, then heads toward a hallway as she says, "Follow me, please."

In the room, Olivia pulls out a chair for Nim and I pull one out for her. Nims gives me a smile and Olivia thanks me with her own soft smile. Duncan glowers from across the table and I just smile at him. I notice Callum's amused smirk at the same time as Duncan. Duncan rolls his eyes and seats himself.

Our server comes in and takes orders. We all know what we want by the time they walk in. I think Olivia's order might have been decided before we arrived. We make small talk while waiting for the food. They are fast here and our food arrives within ten minutes. I am glad, stilted conversation about the rain isn't my favorite. Our server shuts the door as they leave, telling us to open the door if they are needed.

The door closes and Olivia sighs, "I think we know why the church is after me so hard."

Duncan lifts a brow. "And why is that?"

"Because I am half demon."

Duncan chokes a little. "I'm sorry, you're what? I must have heard you wrong."

Callum chimes in, "You heard her right. She is half demon. There is nothing ambiguous about that statement. Unless, are you scared? Worried she'll take your soul or some stupid shit like that?"

I can't help but laugh when he says that. Even as upset as she is, Olivia smiled when he said it. Duncan pulls out his phone and starts tapping away at it. I ask him, "What are you doing?"

He never even looks up as he says, "I'm reporting to Roman. He'll want to know this."

Olivia waves her hand and his phone flies across the room, bouncing off the wall and coming to rest face up. Duncan stands to go after his phone and she says, "You touch that phone and we are fighting."

He freezes in place. "Are you saying you mean to keep this from him?"

Callum's eyes meet mine, and he shakes his head with a frown. Olivia says, "No. I don't keep secrets the way you do. I plan to tell him myself. Not have you run to him like I am hiding something. Fuck, Duncan, do need to have your nose that far up his ass that I can't even tell him my news?"

Duncan sits down and scowls. "No. I was doing my job and getting him the information as quickly as possible."

The room gets a little warmer as Oliva takes a breath. I put my hand on hers and the surprise of it has her looking at me. "You're leaking a little. I thought you would want to know."

She nods, her eyes tearing up. "I do. Thank you. Duncan, I am not your job. And if you need to pass information so badly, you can leave. I don't need this argument. I don't need someone who is more worried about passing information than being here with me while I process the information. It's an asshole move. "

Duncan's face tightens as he nods and says, "Very well. I will see you at the house and in the meantime I will send Niall and some others to you. Enjoy your dinner."

He stands and walks over to collect his phone, all of his body language speaking of deep offense. I would feel some sympathy for him if he wasn't being so disrespectful to Olivia. As it is, I just wish he would leave her in peace rather than chasing her, only to pull another stunt like this when she doesn't conform to the vampire way.

Olivia is rubbing her chest again as he closes the door behind him. The rest of the dinner is tinged with her sadness. We talk to her and she responds, even initiates some of the conversation. Her sadness that his need to tell Roman her news before she could was stronger than his desire to be here with her is a pall hanging over the room. We finish and I smell the blood from Callum piercing his tongue with that sharp tooth again. I wonder if he realizes it's a tell.

We walk out of the restaurant after being told that Duncan paid before he left. And tipped. Olivia seemed a little cheered by that. Niall and two other vampires are waiting outside. He greets Olivia with a smile and a hug. She asks, "Did he already tell Roman?"

Niall replies, "I don't know for sure. My guess would be yes."

She looks at the ground a moment before looking up at me. "Ready to take me home? I need to talk to Roman. Even if he already told him. He doesn't know everything."

"I'll take you anywhere you want to go. "

Niall speaks up then, "Um, we were sent with a car. You are welcome to come with us, Blair. But Roman requested she ride home with us for safety."

I look at Olivia, she says, "It's fine, we can ride with them."

Chapter Six

OLIVIA

I want to believe Duncan cares, but his high-handed attitude is not ok. We all head for the car Niall and the others brought. There are two more vampires waiting at the car. They open the doors for us. It's a bit of a tight fit, but we manage. Nims is sitting on the floor in front of me, leaning onto my lap. Blair is on one side of me, Callum on the other. The stress of the day eases and I find my eyes dropping. I think I could nap for a week or three.

I let my eyes close. I'll just rest them on the way home. Then the world explodes into shattering glass, metal screeching, screams, and pain. Opening my eyes, the first thing I see is Nims face, a hair from mine. She backs away once she realizes I'm okay. Everyone is in disarray. One of the vampires that came with Niall was hit by whatever crushed the car in. He is healing but his arm is going to need to be set properly. Officers snatch the doors open, they lean in, asking, "Is everyone all right? Let's get you looked at by our ECA."

They pull us out of the vehicle and I get a bad feeling. Nims snaps at the one that tries to take my arm. We get out on our own. Almost immediately, an ECA grabs my arm and tugs me toward a med van. It doesn't look exactly like the ones I'm used to seeing racing about. I try to pull away and the man grips my arm harder, saying, "Come on. You need to be looked over."

I snatch my arm away from him and as I do, his jacket slips back, revealing the silver cross strapped to him. Screaming as loudly as I can, I punch him in the face. The scene erupts into violence as the cops attack everyone and I realize they are vampires. Fuck, it's the church people and the vampires they've been working with. Two more men rush toward me. Nims dives at one, biting him right where it makes him scream the loudest. The man is beating at her head, trying to get her to let go of his dick, but Nims is just clamping harder and shaking her head. I step to the side as the other man gets to me, and grabbing the back of his head, I push him toward the ground. His head makes a sickening crunch as it hits the pavement. Other vampires and some witches have run into the fray. I see Duncan running for us, more vampires following him.

Moving closer to Nims, I hit the guy she is biting, watching him crumple to the ground as she releases him. Feeling movement next to me, I turn and my chest explodes in pain as a silver cross plunges into me. I fall to my knees as the man that stabbed me shouts a psalm at me. Nims is pressing against me, howling like she feels the pain.

I didn't think this was how I would die. A light seeps out around the cross, it burns. It's like liquid fire. It's pushing the cross out. I can feel the light spreading through me. Ah fuck, it hurts so much. Is dying always this painful? I feel the cross fall away as Nims presses harder against me. Using what little strength I have, I put my arms around her and hold tight. The pain, oh god, the pain.

Callum

I hear Olivia and Nims screaming, howling in pain as I rip the heart out of one of mother's stooges. Turning, I see her and Nims surrounded by a blinding light, floating a few feet in the air. She is holding tightly to Nims even as Nims clings to her. She is stunning. What is that? Are those? Oh, they will not be happy about that. Especially Duncan. Can't restrain someone if they can literally fly away. Sonofabitch, Nims got wings too. Oh, this is marvelous. Someone hits me and I reach out and snatch them to me, holding them under one arm as I separate head from body.

I glance around and notice that most of the fighting is done. Anyone not fighting is watching Olivia. The humans aren't milling about or taking video anymore; I am guessing the witches took care of that. Thank fuck, because there is no way to spin what is happening to Olivia and Nims. I see Duncan and Roman off to one side, talking as they watch. Looking back at her, I see her wings have finished emerging.

She is floating back to the ground. Blair is just the other side of her, blood dripping down a chin that still doesn't look entirely human. The witches are heading toward her. Dropping the corpse I was still holding, I run over to be at her side when they get to her.

Olivia looks up at me as I stop next to her, careful to avoid stepping on her wings. She says, "Oh, did you die too? I'm sorry."

Crouching next to her, I say, "I didn't die, and neither did you. We are both still very much part of the world."

Blair crouches on her other side, his chin fully human now, if still covered in blood. He says, "You didn't die, love."

The two witches stop before her. The one on the left says, "We would like to transport you to Ailsa now, if you would allow that?"

Olivia nods even as I say, "Not without us."

The witches shrug, and suddenly we are all in the field outside Ailsa's home. So much for warning a vampire before snatching him around magically.

Chapter Seven

OLIVIA

My head feels like it is wrapped in wool. I couldn't have argued with the witches if I wanted to. I was a little surprised to hear Callum say they couldn't take me to Ailsa without them, but maybe it's just my fuzzy brain interpreting things wrong.

The field in front of Ailsa's house is nice. I like it here. Ailsa comes out of her house, a cup and a bowl in her hands. She says, "Drink this, you'll feel better." I accept the cup from her and sip. It tastes of herbs and blood and something else I can't quite define. She smiles softly and says, "It's ok to let her go now. You are both safe. She needs to drink her own brew." I look to my left and I am shocked to see Nims curled up against me.

She seems content to be there and looks as though she isn't feeling super right now, either. Callum plucks the cup out of my hand before I can spill it everywhere. Using both hands, I ease her to her feet. She sits before she is even fully standing. Ailsa sets a bowl before her and she lays down to drink from it. That's when I see them. "Oh. My dog has wings. Nims, you have wings."

Nims is more interested in the dish than my astonishment at her wings. Callum puts the cups back in my hands, making sure I have a hold on it before he releases it. Blair crouches next to me. "Drink up and we'll talk more about wings when you aren't feeling so off."

I nod and sip. It really is an odd taste. I can't quite pin it down. But I keep drinking. Every sip brings me a little more into focus. As if I had slipped outside of the world a little and every sip inched me back into it. I notice my shoulders feel different somehow. Heavier. Once I finish the last of my cup, Ailsa extends her hand towards me. As I pass the cup to her, I feel an odd sensation on my back. Turning my head to look back and see what is touching me, I gasp and nearly fall over when I see the what is behind me.

Blair catches me before I hit the ground. I scramble to stand. "What the fuck?" I twist and stretch to see my back. "Are those wings? Oh fuck. Wings? How?" I notice something else floating behind me. "*Is that a tail?*" I can hear the shrillness in my voice, but I don't care. Reaching behind me, I run a hand across my backside and sure enough, there is a tail sticking out of my pants.

Callum says, "It's a very sexy tail, if that helps any."

I stop and turn to glare at him. He has this smirk on his face and when I glare at him, he just raises his brows suggestively and destroys all the annoyance. I get hold of the tail and bring it round so I can see it. It's a dark blue fading into black. It is kind of pretty. How the hell am I going to be out in public with a tail? And wings? I can't decide if I should be in awe or crash out. I reach back and grab a wing, pulling it forward so I can see it better. It seems to have the same sort of coloring. The tail and the wing are both soft like leather that has been worn a lot. Everyone has been silent while I figure out my new parts.

I should probably say something, but I just need to figure this out for me right now. Looking her way, I see my Nims is curled up, having a nap. Maybe I should have done that instead. No. I need to sort myself and get right with these things. "Ailsa, will we be able to hide these?"

She says, "Yes. If you wish."

How do I move these things? Releasing the tail and wing, I try to move the tail around in front of me without grabbing it. I can feel it moving back there, but it isn't coming round the front. I got it to move. I'll take that for now. What about the wings?

Duncan

Dammit! The fucking witches took off with Olivia. They took Callum and Blair as well, but they can have them. It's Olivia I need to see. I need to know how she is coping after all of this. Make sure Nims is okay and Olivia's magic didn't hurt her.

Roman taps me on the shoulder, and I turn to see him standing behind me. I forgot about him when she disappeared. Shit. He says, "She'll be safe with the witches for now. We need to help get this area cleaned up. Get our people to stack the bod—no. What in the fuck is she doing here?"

Following his gaze, I see Diane and some of her lackeys walking toward us from an alley. I whistle and every vampire that is part of our family focuses on us. When they see Diane's entourage, they draw closer. The witches pause in their cleanup efforts to watch as well. I snatch my phone out of my pocket and start a message to Callum.

Diane notices the other vampires and stops about 6 meters from us. "We just want the girl. She's nothing to you, just an untrained vampire with no manners. Let us take her off your hands."

Roman laughs. "I think the fuck not. She is part of our family. Now that I can warn you publicly, in front of witnesses, you attack another member of my family and we will wipe you off the face of the planet. You can tell the church you are working with that the same goes for them. She belongs to us. I'm surprised that your husband—oh, how insensitive of me to forget. You are no longer married. Your marriage contract became voided when you attacked Olivia and tried to hand her over to the church. Didn't your husband send out a missive with a bounty on you? Am I remembering correctly, Duncan?"

Cracking my knuckles and rolling my shoulders, I reply, "I believe he did. Perhaps we should put Diane in the dungeon until we find out for sure? I've already let Callum know his mother is here. I imagine he is on the phone with his father right now."

Diane looks nervous as the words leave my lips. She licks

her lips and says, "This was your last chance to give her up. You'll regret this."

She turns and runs back toward the alley she emerged from, her people following behind her. More than a few vampires laugh as she runs away.

Chapter Eight

Olivia

We figured out spells to keep the non magical people from seeing my wings. It took us a while because the spells seemed to slide off the wings and tail. It was wildly frustrating till we figured out how to make them stick. We had to use fire and air as the elements, which was its own complication. Either way, we got them disguised. Since riding in Blair's mom's van worked so much better, we decide that is how we are going to get me back home. The witches could transport me, but that isn't always going to be available, and I want other methods of travel. Blair called his mom a few minutes ago and explained the situation. She was thrilled to be able to help. Now, we are all standing near Ailsa's front door, waiting. Ailsa tells me, "You'll get the wings figured out. And you'll both probably be able to fly. It will be great. Few people, or demons, get to fly."

"I am a little excited about that. I'm just feeling a little undone with all the changes hitting me at once."

She pats my arm. "Of course you are. It's a lot. Anyone

would feel overwhelmed with all this. It's not even me and I feel a little overwhelmed by it for you. I can only imagine being in the thick of it all. But you'll get through this. And you will have some new abilities to practice. I'm going to check in with some of the flighted communities and see if we can't find you a someone to help you both figure out flying."

Ashana pulls up just then and we say our goodbyes, hurrying to get in the van. My wings bump the door of the van and it feels like they, along with my tail, suck back into my body. It is the weirdest feeling and I nearly fall back out of the van. Would have, if Callum hadn't caught me. He murmurs, "Retractable, that's handy."

"It feels incredibly weird." He helps me into the van, and Nims jumps in after. She sits next to me, very upright, to keep her wings from being bent. I say, "Nims, I'm going to tap your wings to see if they will retract the way mine did. You need to know, it's going to feel really weird. I don't know a good way to describe it. They kind of suck back into you." She nods her consent and I tap her wing lightly. Her eyes round and she wobbles a bit as the wings retract. I put a hand on her to steady her and she leans into it. I scoot closer and give her a hug while the others get into the van and close the door. Ashana puts it in gear and starts driving.

She is happily telling Blair about various things to do with the shop and I let my mind wander. I have been feeling a simmering anger since I got focused again after the emergence. I wasn't really sure why until Ashana pulled up and waved, never even batted an eye at the fact that I've sprouted wings since the last time she saw me. Blair and Callum insisted on staying with me after, just to make sure

I was ok. The witches took me to the one person who would be able to help me be all right. In the midst of all this, no one has been judgemental.

No anger, no telling me I am terrible. No one has abandoned me. A flash of insight and I know why I am angry. When I struggled after being turned, my family tried to put me through an exorcism. They shunned me. My so-called friends abandoned me and reported me. The only one I have left from that time, the only one that stayed by my side, was Nims. She has been my rock all this time, my companion no matter what. Sometimes my teacher. I couldn't have survived without her. Not with everyone in my life abandoning me.

I'm mad as hell at my parents. At the friends that weren't really friends. I need to know why my parents abandoned me so quickly and have now spent over a decade helping the church try to capture me.

Noticing that we are pulling up to the mansion, I lean forward when Ashana puts her window down. Before I can say a word, she tells the person asking who she is over the intercom, "Tell Roman that Ashana is here to see him."

Immediately the intercom crackles as they say, "Yes ma'am. Go right through."

Blair looks at Ashana with wide eyes and a slack jaw. She shrugs, "We all have a past, son. I was alive for a long time before I chose to have you."

We head directly to Roman's office as soon as we are parked. He greets Ashana with a warm hug. Then he moves to me and asks, "Are you all right?" Tears well up from nowhere and he pulls me into a big hug, patting my back and murmuring, "It's ok. I've got you. Get it all out. We'll make it through this. You are not alone."

I feel Nims sit on our feet and lean on me. I drop one hand down to rest on her head. Her presence is always a great comfort to me. I pull back in horror from Roman when I realize I am crying on his expensive suit. "I'm so sorry, I am probably ruining your suit."

He scoffs, "I'm not worried about the suit. You are much more important to me than any suit I own."

My heart doesn't know what to do with this. Sobbing into his shoulder isn't ideal, but here I am doing exactly that. I've never been more important than anything to anyone until recently and its mind blowing and terrifying. I love all these people so much and any or all of them could be taken away so fast. What if they suddenly decide they hate me? I don't know if I could take it. Finding people that seem to love and accept me? I thought having Nims was me hitting the jackpot.

When the sobs subside, he leads me to a chair; after we pull our feet out from under Nims. Nims quickly follows and Roman presses a handkerchief into my hand after I am seated. I've felt the looming presence of Duncan behind me this whole time, but I just can't deal with him right now. Roman drops to one knee in front of me and says, "Now, tell me all about it. I want to hear everything you want to share."

Everything spills out. The arguments, the attack, the wings, and my feelings. "I think I need to get some answers. I need to go talk to my parents."

Before Roman does more than nod his head in understanding, Duncan blows up. "Absolutely not! You will not go see those people! What in the hell are you thinking? They want you dead. They are helping the church HUNT you." He goes on saying the same thing in five different ways. He winds down and looks to Roman. "Tell her. Tell her that her idea is batshit crazy and she can't do that."

I am still staring at my hand. It looks so small clasped in Roman's. "Duncan. You don't own me and you have no say in what I do."

Roman sighs. "I think you should go. You need answers and your parents are human. They will only be alive for so long. Once they are gone, you won't have any way of getting those answers. I assume the two stooges waiting patiently in the corner plan to go with you?" I turn to look in the direction he indicated and see Blair standing next to Callum, the two of them watching us. They nod in my direction. I turn toward Duncan as Roman says, "You could probably ask her nicely and be allowed to go. If not, between them," he gestures toward Callum and Blair. "And Niall, she will be adequately protected considering as she isn't exactly defenseless herself."

Duncan is fuming. If he were human, I think his face would be bright red. His glare is more disrespect than the vampire society would ordinarily tolerate, but Roman just rolls his eyes and focuses his attention on me. "Where are your wings? You and Nims both had wings last I saw you. Where are they now? Or is it a spell so good you move as though they don't exist?"

I explain how we found out about the wings retracting and he is fascinated. "Come, we should all continue this conversation over dinner. You and Nims haven't eaten all day, have you?"

"Not much, no. We were out to eat, but my appetite was not great."

"It's settled then. Let us all adjourn to the formal dining room and we will eat while we plan."

Blair

Callum might be an asshole for taking Olivia away to Italy, but he's got his priorities right since we brought her back home. When Duncan started shouting at Olivia, he took a step forward, only stopping because I put a hand on his shoulder. I know she won't appreciate either of us dragging him outside to help him understand boundaries. Roman might be ok with it.

Now we've all moved to the formal dining room, and she is sitting next to Roman, Callum on the other side and my mother across from her on Roman's other side. Duncan is in the seat next to my mother. He looks annoyed at being moved further from proximity to Roman and Olivia. The temptation to poke at him is there but, I glance at Olivia; she is fussing with the chair between her and Roman, brought for Nims. She looks frayed. I can see the shadows left on her face from the tears shed on Roman's jacket. A jacket that he is still wearing and has shown zero concern about the state of. His focus has been solely on her and her feelings.

Luckily, jealousy isn't something I am ever going to

bother with. Polyamory is the general way of things in our culture. Women aren't born or made as often and they are treasured, as they should be. The men tend to stay with one woman, regardless of whether there are other women available. Roman would be a strong addition to her collection. Callum is a better addition than he appeared at first. His sense of humor is dry and dark, but isn't punching down. Except with Duncan, but that is Duncan's own fault. Hell, I want to punch down on Duncan. With my fist.

Even now, he is sitting next to my mom and stewing over Olivia's choice. His energy could be better spent supporting her and helping to protect her as she navigates her new abilities. Roman is feeding Nims from his plate as he asks, "Do you have ideas on how we will keep Nims undetected as you seek answers from your parents? US vampires are... less tolerant of changes. They are still trying to prove themselves after all this time. Anomalies are not welcomed."

Olivia says, "I'm not sure. We, the last time we were there, we spent most of our time running from the church. We weren't really visible to most people, and we didn't run into any other vampires. I could easily do that again, but I don't think it would work as well with," she gestures around the table, "a crowd of people. And I think some would not appreciate the camping."

Callum snorts, "She is correct. I don't have the slightest desire to camp anywhere. Even when I was human, camping was not an interest. After a few centuries of luxury, not a chance. I vote we act like the wealthy actors in America. Exclusive hotels and fancy sweatpants paired with large sunglasses. Put a jeweled collar on Nims. Nims, you could pull off regal and spoiled, right?"

In response Nims straightens and looks disdainfully down the table.

Laughing, I say, "She's got the pose. I agree with him. No one will bat an eye at her walking around with her security detail. We'll just order her some pricey versions of the exact clothes she wears, anyway. Yoga pants, t-shirts, and whatever shoes her little heart desires."

Olivia gasps, "I don't need new clothes! My shoes are fine. We can do this without all that."

Roman shakes his head no. "No, they are right. You should go there as a wealthy person. I'll give you a card. The adoption may not have gone through yet, but I still consider you my daughter. I would treat you as such, if you will allow it."

Oh, shit. The whole table went silent when he said that. Olivia is staring at him, mouth hanging open. He is watching her closely. This is really important to him. He means it.

The silence drags on and he starts talking again, his voice still even toned, but with the barest hint of nerves. "I know we haven't known each other that long, but in the short time I have known you, I have come to care about you deeply. You are one of the few people that treats me as an equal. Always. Even as you are obeying a command, I had no choice but to give; it is clear you do it because you chose to. You remind me of the daughter I had a long time ago. She died in childbirth, long before I became a vampire. Before she died, she also followed her own heart and mind. The man she chose was content to follow where she led."

He slants a look at Duncan. It's all I can do to keep from laughing. Callum looks down at his lap for a moment and I know he is having the same struggle.

Olivia, looked a little less flabbergasted, says, "I would be honored to be your daughter." Mischief sparkles in her eyes as she quips, "Does this mean I should call you Dad now?"

Her grin changes as Roman chokes up a little. He swallows and says, "I would love that."

Serious now, she reaches over and places her hand over his. "Then that is what I will call you. Especially when you need reminding that you chose a demon for a daughter."

He laughs, the somber moment gone, and the rest of us join in with laughter and toasts. Except for Duncan. He looks less than thrilled with this new development. I wonder if he can see his control slipping further away?

Chapter Nine

OLIVIA

Fucking wings. How do I get them back out? Turning, I ask Nims, "Have you figured out how to get them back out?"

She is laying on the bed watching me. She shakes her head no and then rests her head on her paws. "Well damn. It's ok. I'll figure this out for both of us. We are long past the time when I should figure some things out for us." I try reaching back and tapping my shoulder blade. Nothing. A little jump. Also nothing. "Wings!" Nims raises a brow at me. "I know, but something has got to work. Wings out!" Nothing. I trip over one of my shoes and the wings pop out, keeping me from falling. "Eeee! I got them out! Now, how did I get them out? Was it because I was falling or the shout as I was going down?"

Nims is sitting up again, watching intently. I tap my wings and shout like I did when I tripped. Not so much as a twitch. Was it the fall? Was it the fear as I fell? What if the wings are connected to my feelings? Everything else seems to be. Excitement fills me at the thought and just like that, wings. I am giddy with the knowledge, but I need to control them better than with just my emotions. "Oh god, what if they pop out while I'm having sex?" Nims barks at me and I tell her, "It's our emotions. I got excited thinking I figured it out, and they emerged. I want to be more in control of them than that, because there will definitely be times when I don't want them popping out because I am stressed."

Nims nods and closes her eyes. I watch the grin appear on her face as her wings pop out. "Ah! Good job! You are so smart! How did I ever get so lucky as to have you in my life?" Crossing the room, I hug her and she leans into it, wrapping her wings around me. My heart is melting. Is there anything in life better than my Nims hugging me back? I think not.

We practice getting our wings to obey us. She hugs me with her wings when she gets them to emerge, and I do the same when it is my turn. Nims is much more adept at it than I am. I am cheering her on when Duncan taps on my door as he walks into my room. "What are we celebrating?"

Nims releases me, and I straighten. "Nims being the most amazing dog ever. She has already mastered her wings. I'm getting there, but slower than she is."

He raises his brows. "Hm, sounds like you should work on it some more before you celebrate?"

"Duncan, I can celebrate her even if I am not there yet. It's ok to celebrate someone else doing a thing before you."

"Or you could wait until you can both celebrate?"

My mood sours. I frown and ask him, "Did you come in here for a reason or did you just smell the joy and come to stomp it out?"

He frowns, as if he doesn't quite understand why I am annoyed with him. "Of course, I didn't come to stomp out your joy. I'm not a monster. I came to see what plans you've made for the trip."

He was there when Roman and I set up the plans for the trip. He knows. Fine, I'll play his game to see where he is going with it. I need the practice. I repeat all the same plans we made with him right there in the room, each one with all its details. "That is pretty much it so far. The clothing he ordered for me will be here tomorrow and we should be leaving within the next day or so."

Duncan sighs. "Are you sure we should fly into a major airport? What if they get access to our flight plans?"

Ah, so the idea is to dissuade me from going. I see. "We talked about this. It will be safer in a crowded airport than an isolated one if they get the flight plans. Duncan, I am going. This trip is happening whether you approve or don't. Would you prefer to not go with me? Roman said it's fine if you stay here. If you can't stand the thought of this trip, stay here. I promise, it will be fine if you stay here. I will be safe. You can keep protecting Roman and I will handle this."

Duncan's face twists and he glares at me. "I don't care about me having to go to the US on this trip. I've been there before. I don't want you to go because you have an entire church organization after you. Let someone else go and get answers from your parents."

"No. This isn't something someone can do for me. Do you not understand that I have to do this? I have to see their faces when they answer my questions. Please try to understand."

"I don't understand. It doesn't make any sense at all why it has to be you. Anyone else could go in your place. We could even send someone in disguised as you."

His blithe dismissal of my reasons infuriates me. "Who are you to decide what can be done? Or what makes sense? Get out Duncan. I'm tired of talking to you."

He takes a step toward me and Nims growls at him. He drops his hands and walks out of the room with a dejected slump to his head and shoulders. I feel no sympathy for him. If anything, I wonder if I should cut him off from me at this point.

Duncan

Roman's office feels a lot smaller when I am here to disagree with one of his decisions. He motions for me to sit as he finishes something on his computer. I take a seat in one of the well-cushioned chairs. I haven't spent much time studying the decor of this room. The walls are a pale gray and the curtains a darker slate. There are bookshelves of darker wood. Each shelf is filled with books of all kinds, fiction and nonfiction. I know he is a devourer of books. He's never been overly picky about the subject.

Looking up, I realize the ceiling is a piece of art. The whole thing is a landscape of a place I am not sure exists. It is beautiful.

"You are the first to have noticed that painting."

"I am? How is that even possible? You have vampires

and various other creatures in here regularly. None of them noticed this?"

"Not one. To be fair, there isn't often a time that people come in here and aren't engaged in conversation about something nearly the instant they walk in."

"I can see that. I believe this is the first time for me and I spend a relatively large amount of time in here with you. Did you do this?"

Roman nods, "I did. But you came in here for something other than admiring my ceiling work. What can I help you with? Wait, shouldn't you be packing?"

"I am here in the hope that I can convince you to stop this idiocy from moving forward. She should be here where we can protect her."

Roman sighs, "I thought, hoped, that you had come to terms with this. Why are you so hell-bent against this trip?"

"Because it puts everyone in danger. Everyone on the trip will be in danger just so Olivia can get some questions answered by her human parents. They shouldn't even know she is alive by now, much less be seeing her completely unchanged from the last time she saw them. And the church is probably going to attack. We've just had a close call with them attacking. We wouldn't have won had we not had numbers on our side. They won't under-estimate us again. You know this. Why are you allowing this to happen?"

"This has to happen, Duncan. She needs the closure and her parents have information about her origins that she needs now more than ever. She needs to know why the church is after her. That is the only way for us to find the right way to stop them from hunting her without annihilating the entire organization. You know we can't do that. It would expose vampires to the world of humans."

"We could if we hired humans to do the killing. Or plant information so that the human governments of the world tear the organization into shreds. There are so many ways we could do this that would not endanger vampire secrecy. And honestly, what good will come of her parents answering questions? She'll know exactly how terrible they really are? Roman, lives could be lost just so she can have her little side quest."

Roman shakes his head. "Lives will be lost no matter what she does. They attacked her in broad daylight in the middle of an intersection. Do you really think they will stop hunting her any time soon? This trip, dangerous as it is, buys us time. Time that we need. I am preparing for a war. Her trip is needed for more than one reason and if you weren't so wrapped up in yourself, you would know that."

"What? I am thinking of her safety!"

"If it was about her safety, you would ask about extra security and research ways to get her through this as safely as possible. You are trying to control her because you are afraid of losing her. I don't know if you've noticed, but trying to control her is pushing her away and you are going to lose her because you can't manage your fear. I expected better of you."

God dammit. Roman doesn't understand. And I don't know how to make him understand. "I disagree, but I need to get packed if I am going to go with her. I still think this is a bad idea, but I yield to your wisdom. Thank you for hearing me."

Roman nods and turns back to his computer as I stand and leave his office.

Chapter Ten

We land in Florida and the anxiety sets in. Immediately, the accents are different from the lilt of the Scots that I quickly became accustomed to within a year of arriving. The southern twang grates on my tenuous control. Even Nims seems less comfortable here. But maybe she is picking up on my emotions.

We are supposed to head directly for my parents' house. Get this over with. Before we even leave the airport, Blair, Callum, Duncan, and Niall have talked among themselves like I wasn't right here and decided to book a room at some rich beachfront hotel. They have a large rental suv brought up for us. I am continually amazed at the things money can do.

We speed away, driving over toward the beach and pulling into one of those places so grand I used to be afraid of looking at it too much. Everything is so bright and white here. I am more than grateful for the huge famous person sunglasses that Roman bought for me. The whole suitcase I brought is filled with things he picked. I gave him my sizes, and he apparently did some research as he shopped. I have a feeling that more clothing is going to appear in my rooms at his house.

My eyes bug out a little as they stop to obtain valet parking. That is wild. I've never stayed in a place with that. I watch the large suv glide off toward some hidden parking area as Nims crowds my legs, her nerves as frayed as mine.

They have us in a suite of rooms, technically one room, but way bigger than I thought possible in a hotel. Each of us has our own bedroom in this place, with a central area that is bigger than my first apartment. I can't believe how fast all this went through. I think it took maybe twenty minutes. It's all seemed a little surreal for me. I feel like I've just been catching certain scenes and gone for other parts.

Next thing I know, Nims and I are out on a mostly deserted beach, Niall at my side and the other three not far behind, talking in quiet but angry tones. Niall looks at me, "Ah, you're back. Maybe you'll stay with us this time?"

"Yes, at least, I hope so. This has been a lot, coming back here. I didn't expect it to be the shock that it is. Did I miss anything important?"

He shakes his head no. "Nothing but those three arguing about how best to handle this."

"What options have they come up with?"

"Well, Callum and Blair are mostly in agreement about giving you some time here to adjust. They only disagree about how long. Duncan, well, I think you know what his idea is."

"He wanted to get back on the plane and take me home."

"Yes."

"I'm not going home until I talk to them. This place, it holds a lot of memories. Most of them aren't good and they kind of hit me all at once when I heard people talking in that southern twang I haven't heard in so long."

Niall nods, "I understand. It hasn't been long enough for the scar to be faded. Or maybe it has, but with the renewed attacks, you are more sensitive to it. How are you feeling now?"

"Better. Nims and I, we spent some good times here on the beaches. There are a lot of little places to hide and as long as the cops don't see you going in there, you can sleep safely to the sound of the wind and waves. We got sneaky for a little while. We had a little cubby built into a dune. Some stolen craft products, and it looked like just a regular dune. It worked well until they found us again. We had to run. We spent so much time running away from them. I don't want to run anymore, Niall."

Niall glances back at the others, still furiously whispering at each other. "I think, and this isn't certain, but I get the impression that Roman is working on making sure you have nothing to run from ever again. You know, I've seen pictures of his daughter. You bear a very strong resemblance to her painting. In fact, considering paintings almost never make a spot on replica, you may look even more like her than I know. I would bet that Roman remembers her face well and I don't see him as one to exaggerate. What I know for sure is that according to the records I've seen, and I love old records reading, Roman has claimed no one as a family member of any sort. Not even informally. He plans to not only adopt you into the vampire family, but publicly claim you as his daughter."

"He, really? He plans to publicly claim me?" I feel my eyes sting and I know they are red with blood tears unshed.

"He does. And that is part of why I think he is working in the shadows to eliminate the threat against you. He lost his daughter a long time ago, and I think he would have changed her if she had lived long enough for him to be changed. As it is, he still watches over her descendents."

"Still? They have to be so many generations removed from her and he still watches over them?"

"Yes. They have no idea. If they run into trouble or something, a miraculous grant appears or something. They are fully human and his only weakness. The only people that know about them are his enforcers and now you."

"I'll keep his secret. I am honored that he would consider me his daughter. Say, has he been getting those pieces of art back to their owners? I know they have been disappearing."

Niall laughs, "Yes. He has been returning them to the peoples they belong to. Some of them he has replicas made for himself. But he sends the original back to the people they came from. His only stipulation to them is that they do not reveal how they got it back. Even if they revealed their benefactor, they would have to follow a long trail to get back to Roman."

I stop walking. All is silent behind us. Looking down, I check in with my Nims. She grins up at me, and I know she is okay too. "I think I am ready to go back to the room for now."

Niall looks back at the others, "Have you lot finished your... discussion?"

Callum smirks, "We have."

Blair smiles as Duncan sighs and looks to the ocean. "We are going to spend however long Olivia decides she needs here before we go visit her parents. Once that is done we will leave as quickly as possible because it is goddamned hot and stinky here."

I laugh. "I like the conclusion of your discussion. I think I would like to go back to the room now and eat, if everyone is good with that?"

Callum

We get back to the suite after grabbing some food down by the beach and Olivia retreats to her room. She slams the door in Duncan's face as he was still attempting to talk her into going home. His face when he saw me watching was almost rewarding. Except she is hiding away from everyone because he was hounding her about going home.

"I'm going downstairs and have a few drinks. You've got my number if you need anything."

Niall and Blair nod, Blair waving me off. The elevator is less than silent or smooth. If it plummets to the ground, I'm biting someone. It grinds to a shaky halt on the ground floor; the doors opening to release me into a group of drunken fools waiting to go to their rooms and fuck with abandon in ways they can't when sober because it would be too dirty.

I grab a seat at the bar, ordering a drink and shrimp. Sipping on my drink, I see a couple of men with the collars of holy men walk in and seat themselves at the bar. I continue to sip my drink as though I haven't noticed them, but my every sense is focused on them. One grumbles about the lack of cooperation from the front desk. The other says, "Maybe she isn't checked in and just came to visit someone. We know she is still here. No one has seen her leave. Just think of the rewards he'll grant us if our team catches her. We're guaranteed to move up in the organization. High up."

The first snaps, "Or she is, and the desk clerk just won't come off the information. Hopefully Ed will have more luck talking with him. I just want to drag him out back and send him to God now. We should have grabbed her when we saw her at the airport."

The second one says, "We had other things we had to do right then. At least we were able to have someone follow her here and make sure they saw if she left."

The bartender brings my shrimp over; I ask for a box and the check. He grabs a paper tray I can take with me and dumps my shrimp into it. Not the most elegant of places. I pay my tab and thank him with a generous tip. Downing the rest of my drink, I stand and stroll slowly back to the elevator. Listening all the while for those two men getting up to follow me. I see their friend at the front desk. He is badgering the clerk, who is telling him that he will call the cops if he does not leave right now.

It takes every ounce of willpower to walk at a normal pace back to the room. Two women walking past me try to chat me up. The fumes from the alcohol they've had are horrid. Smells like poorly processed cheap whiskey. "Thank you, ladies. I'm flattered but not interested. Have a night."

They are offended and huff away with clouds of boozey sweat left in their wake.. I continue down the short hall that seems incredibly long. Arriving at our suite, I let myself in, looking back the way I came as I do. No one there, the ladies made it into the elevator and no one else has come up here.

In the suite, I head straight for her door. She says, "Go away Duncan," when I knock. "I'm not Duncan and we have a problem."

The door opens to reveal Olivia in a t-shirt that reaches her upper thighs and Nims standing next to her. "What problem?"

Dragging my eyes up from those luscious thighs, I tell her what I saw and heard downstairs. By the time I finish, the other three have come over to listen.

Duncan says, "This is exactly what I was talking about. We need to get out of here and go home, where you will be safe."

Olivia glares at him as her wings spring forth from her back, tail swishing in anger behind her. "Duncan, one more time and you can go back home alone. I'm done listening to your attempts to control me. If you don't have anything else to offer to the conversation beyond going home, I suggest you keep quiet."

Duncan walks away, fuming. Blair sighs. "I think we do need to leave here." Olivia looks at him with venom in her eyes and he holds his hands up in a placating manner, "I just mean the hotel. They are going to go door to door if they can't convince the desk clerk to tell them where you are. We should go stay elsewhere."

Olivia seems satisfied with his explanation. "The places in Lake City, they aren't like this. Are you all going to be ok with that? Staying in a regular hotel?"

Niall laughs. "I think we can manage. All right, everyone pack up. Duncan, if you could sneak down and collect the keys from the valet station, that would be very useful. Don't bring it round front. Just get in and wait for my message. I'll pack your things."

Duncan nods and leaves the room without another word. Olivia grabs her computer and books us rooms in Lake City. Seating myself next to her, I look over and realize; she isn't on a hotel website. She sees me noticing and puts a finger to her lips. Nodding, I can't help but be amused. She is booking us a house somewhere in the woods. With a gate. Duncan will be so happy. I bet it even has a security system. Once she has the confirmation email, she closes her laptop. "We won't be able to check in till tomorrow. Do you think it would be safe enough to stay here one more night?"

"Possibly, but Duncan is going to be mad if we don't leave here tonight."

She sighs, her eyes rolling. "We can stay in one of the Lake City hotels for a night. I... I just don't want to run into people I used to know."

"You could always bite them. Or let Nims bite them. I'm sure she would enjoy it."

A nod and a quiet woof from Nims makes Olivia smile. She sets her computer to the side and stands. "I'll go pack."

Nims follows her and I move to my room to get my bag packed.

My bag is small and light. Moments later, I have my bag in hand as I wander into her room, after a detour to pack up her computer and sling the bag over my shoulder. She is pulling a pair of sweats over her gorgeous ass and I know I should look away, but I just can't.

She notices me in the mirror and says, "It's rude to spy on people."

"I wasn't trying to be sneaky about it, so it wasn't spying. I was appreciating the view."

Chapter Eleven

BLAIR

What in the hell does Duncan have in his bags? I offered to carry them, but I am having second thoughts. How is his bag heavier than Olivia's? About the time I start down the stairs, I stop because I hear someone banging on the doors to the rooms we just left. Fuck. Setting the bags down on the landing, I run back up the stairs and quietly wedge a knife in the top edge of the door. It won't hold forever, but it will slow them down. Back down the stairs and I grab the bags, hustling to catch up to everyone.

Whispering, I let them know we would have had company if we had stayed upstairs. Everyone moves a little faster. At the bottom of the stairs, Niall peeks out the door. Poking his head out further, he checks the area thoroughly before saying, "Come on, Duncan has just pulled up. Maybe if we hurry, they won't realize we've gone for a time."

Olivia and Nims dive into the truck. We stow all the bags and climb in. Duncan pulls away from the curb, quiet and smooth, like it were any other day. Oliva and Nims sit up once we make it to the interstate. Even with the tinted windows, she didn't feel safe sitting up.

Duncan is gripping the steering wheel like it offends him. That guy really has to calm down. Callum is reading one of Olivia's books, chuckling at something I'm sure was meant to be dramatic or horrifying.

Olivia and Nims are huddled into each other, both looking grim and sad. Niall is the only one I can't see well, but he is turned to face toward the back and watch Olivia. "Olivia, maybe you and Nims should have something to eat?"

"No. There isn't anything for miles. At least, nothing I want to eat. Even when I was human, the space between Jacksonville and Lake Shitty was a sort of no-man's-land for food. You can get fireworks though. Probably. I guess it's still open. There used to be a hole in the wall strip club through here too, but that closed down because the owners did too much coke and weren't paying the bills."

Callum gasps from the seat behind us, "They fucked up a strip club? For shame. Those places are massively easy to run in a place like this, as long as you have someone to handle the dramatics bound to come from some of the dancers."

Olivia nods, "Yes, they did. But that is kind of exemplary of the area. This place is not good. I hated it when I had to live here. I hate having to come back. I'll be glad to go back home to Inverness."

Duncan chimes in with, "We could leave tonight."

Olivia snarls, "That's enough out of you. I will tell you

when I am ready to leave. Until then, you don't need to speak to me."

"Goddammit, Olivia! I just want you safe."

"You've made that perfectly clear. You've also made it perfectly clear that your concern for my safety should take priority over anything I want or need for me. And I am real fucking sick of it. Keep talking and you can travel without me. Roman gave me this card and his fucking number so that I would not have to worry about your opinion. Shut your fucking mouth or so help me, I will call him myself."

Niall puts a hand over Duncan's mouth before he can spew whatever retort he had boiling up. "Duncan, she asked you nicely. She told you in various ways. Please do not make me call Roman and have you recalled home. Which I assure you will go over so much better than an angry Olivia calling him."

Niall removes his hand and Duncan gasps, "You wouldn't!"

Olivia says, "If he doesn't, I will."

Duncan grumbles something unintelligible and I try not to laugh. "So, is there food in Lake City that you'll be willing to eat?"

She shrugs, "Not this late. I can wait until things are open again. By the time we get there, we'll just have to get a room and chill there until we can go find food. We won't be able to check into the place I reserved till late afternoon. But we could buy groceries at the better grocery once it is late enough in the morning. It is a major chain in Florida and the only one that is reliably good no matter what part of Florida you happen to be in."

"What? You mean the rest aren't reliably good?"

Olivia snorts, "Not even close. Honestly, Lake City has a reputation for ruining chains. Went without an ice cream chain for years because the employees embezzled all the money. The restaurants start out decent but most quickly go to shit. It's like the black hole where all good things come to die."

The grumbling up front gets louder for a minute, but Niall clears his throat and it subsides. We get to the area and Olivia directs Duncan on where to go for a room. She gives Niall her card, and he goes in to book a room for us. Duncan stares into the night while we wait. His jaw is so tight I wonder how his teeth aren't crushed with the strain. Olivia watches people out the window, her face a mask. I've never seen her so expressionless before. How bad is this place that it does this to her?

Niall comes back and we decide to leave most of the bags in the truck as we aren't staying here long. Olivia says, "No electronics get left in here. Not even bags that look similar to computer bags. Too many desperate people here."

Fucking hell. We all follow Niall. He leads us to the suite on the top floor. It isn't as big as the last one, but it is larger than a regular hotel room would be. Olivia and Nims settle in on the couch, Nims laying between Olivia's stretched out legs while Olivia's laptop is on her upper thighs. Olivia is typing furiously. If I had to guess, someone is dying gruesomely in one of her books right now.

Duncan took over a spot on the bed. Laying on his back and staring angrily at the ceiling. I decide I would rather sit on the floor near her than anywhere else for the next few hours as we wait for this sleepy town to wake up.

Callum

Blair seats himself on the floor in front of where Olivia is typing furiously and that honestly looks like one of the better places to sit. Niall has the chair and Duncan on the bed. No one wants to be near him while he has such a shit attitude. I walk over and sit on the floor by her legs and Nims. Nims lifts her head and gives my neck a lick before flopping back down.

I guess she approves.

I've been reading one of Olivia's books and thoroughly enjoying it. But now, knowing as much as I do about her, I wonder how much of what I read is an altered reflection of things she went through? The part where her heroine lives in the woods for a time, I know she did that. I believe she wasn't so prepared as her heroine was. More unhoused than camping.

If I understand correctly, these church people have been chasing her pretty much since I turned her and forgot about her. I wonder if it would have changed their pursuit of her if I had been there to take her away? If Diane hadn't set me up to be nearly killed by that family, which I was supposed to be having a diplomatic meeting with; she could have been spared that.

Immersing myself in her book, the next time I look up is when Olivia closes her laptop. Her expression never changes as she says, "We should go now. It is ten and everything should be open. I want some coffee."

Niall asks, "Should we stop in the lobby for some coffee?"

"No, they closed that hours ago and their coffee is not good." She stuffs her computer in her bag as Nims stands and stretches. Blair and I stand and do our own stretching. Thank fuck for being a vampire. I don't think a human could stand hours of sitting on the floor like that. We head out, Duncan silent the entire time. That man can sulk with the best of them.

Olivia directs us to a small drive thru coffee shop, telling us it was the best coffee available here, and that probably hasn't changed any more than the rest of this place. Next stop is the one grocery chain.

Some woman sees three men following Olivia and says, "Whore. Go back to where you came from."

Olivia turns, looks her up and down. Then she takes off her glasses and says, "Ruthie, considering what you and your children get up to, I don't think you should be the first one casting stones."

The woman gasps, "How dare you!"

"Shut up. Your son is a predator in prison. I heard your health isn't great. Seems your gods didn't appreciate how you defended him."

"Fuck you. Stupid whore."

"Fuck you twice, Ruthie. I hope you continue to receive everything you deserve."

The woman storms off and another person claps. When Olivia looks toward them, they give her a grin and a thumbs up. She smiles politely and nods as she pushes the cart forward to continue shopping.

We didn't see the other lady for the rest of the

shopping, but a manager came to find us and tell Olivia that she had to be polite to the other customers. Olivia sighs, "David, get bent. I'm here for five minutes and you of all people want to defend Ruthie to me? Fuck off. I'm finishing my shopping and then I will leave. You'll never see me again. Now go away. God, I hate small towns."

David is left stunned and staring as she moves on. This is insane. What the hell kind of place is this that so many people are comfortable speaking that way to people they don't know? Olivia has us in line at the checkout. Some old woman is staring at her, but she is unbothered. I think she even has her nose in the air a little. This is wild. I wonder if she knows the old woman? She obviously doesn't like her.

Olivia's cashier gets us rung up and out the door in record time. Olivia long-legs it across the lot to the truck like her tail is on fire. She has the groceries in and is getting into the truck within a minute. Exchanging a look with Blair, I get in as he does the same.

Niall tells Duncan, "Let's go. Olivia, you said we could get in the place at noon if we paid an extra fee?"

She nods. "Yes, let me call them. There are entirely too many assholes out today."

One quick phone call later and we are headed to the place she booked. It is in a swamp. I hope it isn't small. We round a curve in the driveway and a spacious home comes into view. Oh good.

Chapter Twelve

OLIVIA

We spent a night in the rental house, so I could decompress more than anything. The shopping trip was unreal. So many people I used to know. Of course, I feel like one person I know from here is too many.

Today. Today we are going to see my parents. I know they are home. They are always home on Mondays.

Pulling up to my parents' house, I kind of want to throw up. Nims stays pressed up against me. She remembers this place. They all exit the vehicle and go to the door with me. I didn't really expect that, but I'm glad they did. I knock and my mother answers the door. She is shocked to see me, her eyes round and her mouth hanging open for a moment. She looks around, checking to see if anyone is watching. She says, "Come in, before someone sees you. Who are all these men with you? My God, how far you have fallen."

We go in and she leads us to this picture perfect living

area. It hasn't changed even a little since the last time I was here. She demands, "Why are you here?"

I tell her, "I need answers. Who is my father? I know it isn't Harold."

Mother looks very uncomfortable. She starts with denial. "Of course he is. I wouldn't step out on my marriage."

Sighing, I tell her, "I know he isn't my father. Why won't you do this one thing for me? Just tell me the truth. Then I'll leave and you won't have to worry about your neighbors seeing me and how low I have fallen ever again."

My father, or the man I thought was my father, walks in then. He looks different. Haggard, defeated. He nearly cries when he sees me. "Olivia, how are you?" After a look from mother, he pulls himself together. "So, what brings you and your friends here? I see you got another dog like the one you had."

I hate this. Hate the pretending. The fake. "Look, I know you aren't biologically my father. I'm trying to find out who I am descended from. Would you please help me with this one thing and I will go away? I won't darken your door ever again."

His laugh is sad and short. He looks at my mother and says, "If you don't tell her, I will."

My mother says, "You tell her at your own peril."

He nods. Looks back at me, "Let's go somewhere else. She's probably already called them. They'll be on their way here now."

We file out and load up in the truck. I tell Duncan, "Just keep driving. Don't stop anywhere."

The man I thought was my father sits in the seat next to

me. I never dreamed I would have to ask questions like this. But here goes. "Where, who am I descended from?"

He sighs. "Technically, me and your mother. In reality, I allowed myself to be possessed so that your mother could have the ranking in the church that she craved more than anything."

Olivia gasps, "What?"

He tells me the whole sordid story. How much he loved my mother and would have done anything for her. Even sell his soul so long as she would love him. The church has paid them very well over the years to have her and raise her. How they were in a lot of trouble when she took off and the church couldn't claim her power.

"You mean sacrifice me for my power?"

"I was assured that they would only take your power, not your life. I swear I didn't know they planned to kill you. Oh god, she did. That's why she always had that little smirk when I said I would be glad when this was over and we could all go on with our lives. She knew you would be dead."

"I think you are right. She always knew. And I never mattered even a little to her. Where do you want to be dropped off at? We can't take you back to your house. They'll be on us long before we get to your neighborhood. Thank you for telling me. I appreciate it. I needed to hear it from one of you."

He says "It doesn't matter where, pick a place. They'll find me no matter what."

"You could come with us. We would take care of you."

He says, "No. They know your powers have come in

and they don't expect we will be able to catch you. We were supposed to delay you."

We let him out at a store. I get out of the truck and walk around to where he stands. "Thank you. I know this is going to cause you problems. Are you sure you won't come with us?"

He says, "No. I'm going to face them. It is what I need to do. I should never have agreed to this. I loved her so much. You are a miracle, no matter how you came to be. Don't let them get you. You deserve better than we ever gave you."

I nod and hug him one last time. Releasing him, I walk back to my side of the truck and get in, a cold feeling in my bones telling me that he will be dead before the sun goes down.

Both the doors closed, Duncan steers the truck back into traffic.

Blair

I climb over the seat to sit next to her once we pull away from the store we left her father at. She looks at Duncan and says, "Now you can take me home."

I wrap an arm around her and she cries into my chest, great heaving sobs.

Duncan says, "We have company."

Looking around, I see there are three cars surrounding us. The one in front hits their brakes and Duncan shouts, "Hold on!" He snatches the wheel to the right and guns it.

The sound of cars scraping against each other as he creates a space is loud in the sudden silence. The cars are chasing us now. We quickly realize we can't outrun them here. Olivia says, "Take the next exit. There isn't much here and we can find a deserted spot to take care of them." Duncan swerves off the exit and never stops at the end of the ramp, drifting around the corner.

Duncan stomps on the brakes as one car cuts in front of us and slams their brakes. As soon as we are stopped, men with silver crosses, stakes at the bottom, pour out of the cars. They surround the truck. One of the men shouts, "Send out the sacrifice and the rest of you can go!"

Nims growl is loud in the van. We exchange glances and Duncan puts his window down just enough to tell them, "We are all coming out. Surely we can talk this through." The men agree, some of them smiling triumphantly.

Duncan, myself, Niall and Callum all get out on the right. Olivia gets out with Nims, the two of them behind the four of us.

Duncan says, "Surely you all are reasonable fellows. How about we give you a bunch of money and you just drive off? Tell them you couldn't get us to stop the truck and we went off roading. You'll have money and we can carry on with our business. Everyone wins."

Their leader, tapping his stake against the palm of his hand, says, "Or we could kill all of you in his name and take her back to him so that she can do her duty as she was created to do. And we can take all your money once you all are dead. She belongs to us. You aren't leaving here with her."

Nims growl matches my own as Callum, flicking that

tooth with an already bleeding tongue, asks, "Are you boys sure that's the way you want to go?"

The lead screams, "Get them!"

Something hot pushes past me, but I don't have time to look as two men come at me with those silver stakes. My wolf nature rises and I change partly. Enough to horrify the men as I grab one by the cross he planned to stab me mith and sling him against the truck. The other one, I snatch him in close and bite him, tearing away the flesh of his shoulder and neck. Spitting it out, I push him away. His screams are ear piercing. The one I threw into the truck stands on wobbly legs, looks at me and vomits on his own shoes. I reach out with one hand to punch him in the jaw. He falls to the ground in a heap.

Turning, I see Callum drinking from one and holding another at arm's length by the throat. That one manages to stab Callum, and he stops drinking long enough to shout in pain.

Snatching the one that stabbed him out of his hand, I rip his arm off and beat him with it. Another one runs up behind me and stabs me in the back with one of those fucking crosses. They hurt like hell and I use the arm still in my hand to knock him away. Unfortunately, that leaves the cross in my back, but I've had worse pain. Turning around to finish off the little backstabber, I realize that Olivia and Nims aren't behind us anymore. Fuck, where are they? Hitting the guy hard enough to knock him out, I look around and find them almost immediately. She is back to tail with Nims. They both have their wings out and are using them as weapons.

The two of them move as if they were one. It is

beautiful. But they've fought enough. Stepping on and over bodies, I snatch up the one swinging at Nims and bring his back down over my knee. I feel a crunch as his spine breaks over my knee and the light leaves his eyes. Nims has already turned to help with the two before Olivia, and with the numbers evened out, they are making short work of the two men.

Duncan and Niall, being toward the front of the vehicle, ended up fighting more of them at first. But that changed as they decided to try the rest of us and died for their troubles. I see one of them trying to crawl toward a vehicle. Walking over, I kick his head for a field goal. The wet crunch is loud in the sudden silence and getting my boot stuck in his head wasn't part of the plan.

Shaking my foot doesn't dislodge it either. Dammit. Looking around, I don't see anything that would work to push it off my foot. Callum says, "I think I can help, hold still."

No sooner than he says still, I feel a ripping from my back and roar with the pain. "Son of a bitch, you could have warned me. I forgot it was there."

Callum walks to the side of me with a grin, "Yeah, it seemed like your body was healing around it. But the blunt end should do well for getting that mess off your shoe."

He uses the cross end to shove the head off my boot and my boot is going to need a lot of cleaning. Fuck. "Thanks. I'm just going to use some dirt over here to get some of this off. I don't want it in the truck with us."

Callum snorts. "I don't think a little brain is going to be the worst thing in the vehicle. Or on it if you consider what Duncan did to make a space."

Chapter Thirteen

OLIVIA

Looking around at all the bodies and Blair's shoe, I feel shaky. My stomach does a weird turn and next thing I know, I'm vomiting on the ground next to a body. Super.

This day just gets better and better. Once I am feeling more composed, I tell them, "There is a cell phone tower down the road. If we park their cars in front of the gate, they'll be ignored until the tech or someone needs to get into the site, then they'll be towed. It could be weeks before they are noticed, depending on when the site is in need of service or an upgrade. Especially if we toss the bodies into the woods here."

The five of us make quick work of the bodies. Duncan, Nims, and I get in the truck while Niall, Callum, and Blair each get in a car and drive it to the tower site. Duncan stops in the road and let them walk out to the truck. The lack of traffic here is really working out for us. Only one car has passed us and it reeked of weed. They are not telling anyone they were here for any reason.

Turning in the rental is... interesting. They have questions and Duncan tells them there was a wreck. They stop asking questions after he produces a large wad of money and says, "We really need to go. This wreck was not accidental, someone targeted us and we would very much like to go home now. My friend here," he gestures toward me, "has some stalkers that are very upset with her lack of interest in them."

The attendants are suddenly very helpful, and we are back in the waiting plane in record time. The flight crew was ready to go as soon as we boarded. I wonder if Duncan called them this morning?

The four of them take turns sitting next to me, obviously trying not to overwhelm me or leave me fully alone with my thoughts for now.

I appreciate the thought. My brain is dwelling on the man I once believed was my father. I'm fairly certain he gave up his life by telling me what he did. I wish he would have come with us. It feels like I understand so much more about how he interacted with me now.

Lost in thought, I don't even notice Blair until he taps my shoulder and says, "You need to eat."

I accept the sandwich and bag of blood; I know Nims won't eat if I don't. And while I am willing to ignore my stomach, I don't want that for her. He sets her food down in front of her where she lays at my feet. She looks up at me and I nod, unwrapping my sandwich.

He asks, "Do you want to talk about it?"

"No, I think I need to just feel it. Do you see any way I could have changed things for him?"

He shakes his head no. Nodding, I say, "I am pretty certain he is going to die for what he shared with us."

Blair says, "Yes. He knew what he was choosing."

Nims presses into my leg. "I need to grieve him. To release him. Even if I see him in the future, he'll just be a puppet run by that demon. I don't want to be confused about what to do if that should happen. I don't want to risk your lives because I couldn't sit with the grief. It sucks. But I just need to be sad about it for a while. I figure a long flight is as good a place as any. Possibly a better place for a lot of reasons."

Chapter Fourteen

Duncan

Roman was exceedingly happy to have Olivia back in Scotland, where she belongs. They spent hours talking alone. The only interruptions were people bringing them food. If it wasn't Roman, I would feel a way about the exclusion. But he is the father she never had, and she lost the only one she knew because he did the one good thing he could do for her. Thank fuck she was finally ready to go home after that. Even if it is probable that they found us because of him.

She's still sad, though she keeps it mostly hidden. I need to stop focusing on her right now. I have to pay attention to the conversation at hand, which I have been doing poorly at. Roman and Ailsa have been discussing the war they feel is coming.

Ailsa says, "We'll need to figure out a way to mark the ones that aren't part of your family. My witches wouldn't recognize your entire family on sight."

Roman smiles, "I'm working on a little surprise for

that. I thought it might be an issue. I'll let you know once I've got it all sorted. In the meantime—"

He stops at a knock on the door. Walking over, I open it a small bit, prepared to tell whoever it is to come back later. Olivia is on the other side of the door. Pushing down my surprise, I tell her, "Sorry, he's in a meeting. You'll have to come back later."

Olivia says, "Yeah, I know. I'm here for the meeting."

Roman calls out, "Olivia, we've been waiting for you. Duncan let her in. Olivia, please catch Ailsa up on what you learned on your trip. I have shared none of it because it is your story, but I think she needs to know all of it."

Olivia walks past me and seats herself in the chair next to Ailsa, after hugging her. She immediately launches into telling her about the trip and her parents. I don't understand why Roman didn't let me know she was coming to the meeting. Why she didn't let me know? I spoke to her this morning.

Olivia wraps up her story, and Ailsa says, "Oh honey, that must've been hard. Are you ok?"

Olivia swallows and nods, "Mostly. I am still grieving him, or grieving the parent I could have had in a different world. I'm ok though."

Roman nods, a proud smile on his face. "Olivia, I think you should know. The city is crawling with Italian vampires and Southich Baptist hunters."

"Hunters?"

"Yes, hunters. I've been investigating their organization, and that is what they call the ones that they keep sending after you. They are stronger than the average person because they are juiced up on some concoction. I haven't quite found what that is, but we are working on it. I think I need to lure a few more hackers into the vampire world. The vampires have all come here at least once, their eyes roaming the house, I suspect, looking for a glimpse of you. It is a safe bet that they know you have returned. The visits have stopped."

Ailsa snorts, "Morons. They should have continued the visits and pretended they knew nothing. Now we know they'll move soon."

Roman chuckles. "Indeed, I would have done the same. Keep them guessing. I want you to stay within the walls of the estate, if you would, Olivia?"

She nods. Doesn't even fight him on it. What the hell? She says, "I will." Then she looks directly at me as she says, "Knowing what is out there, I wouldn't want to endanger anyone."

What does she mean by that? I told her things... mostly.

For the rest of the meeting, Roman and Ailsa talk about the logistics of all the family members coming into town while I watch Olivia. I wonder what else she has neglected to tell me?

Callum

Inverness is a darker, colder climate than Italy, but on days like this, I can see the appeal. The sun is out, and it is a dry day. Even the mist is burned off. The garden is a glorious spot with a variety of flowers that I feel certain are supported by magical means. Olivia's books are engrossing.

Some of the scenes hit so hard even I need to stop a moment and appreciate them. To appreciate the pain, which she must have gone through to come up with something like this.

Staring off into the depths of the garden, I am lost in thought until something moves into my field of vision. Focusing, I see Olivia and Nims at her side. Scanning the rest of the garden, I see Duncan following her. He appears to be hanging back enough that she won't notice him.

Standing and stretching, an idea occurs to me. Duncan will hate it. Which makes it even more appealing. Tweaking his temper gives me joy. I move to take a more circuitous route to meet with Olivia, picking flowers as I go. Just as I pluck the final flower for the bouquet, they come around a corner. Nims spots me immediately and I smile at her as I put the flowers behind my back.

Her answering grin before she pokes Olivia with her nose is wild. I never thought to meet a dog so smart as she is. I know she saw the bouquet and knew it was for Olivia. I don't think anyone else would deserve the loyalty of so intelligent a dog the way that she does. Olivia looks in the direction Nims points with her nose and she smiles when she spots me walking toward them.

As she draws near, I pull the flowers from behind my back with a flourish and a bow, saying, "For you, my lady."

Nims sniffs them first, and after she nods her approval, Olivia reaches out and takes them. Her hands touch mine for the briefest of moments, but it sets me on fire with longing. Pushing my tongue into my canine, I straighten. The pain and blood keep me centered. I watch as she breathes in deeply with her face buried in the flowers. Then she looks at me and throws her arms around me. Nims rushes over to press against the two of us, not willing to be left out. Bringing one arm up around her, I put the other down on Nims head and give her a scratch.

Olivia says, "How did you know I love getting flowers? Thank you!"

My cold heart warms with her joy. "I didn't, but I hoped they would make you smile."

She squeezes me tighter. I absolutely must give her flowers as often as possible. I notice Duncan off to the side, arms crossed and rolling his eyes at me. I give him the biggest smile I can muster and flip him off with the hand on Olivia's back.

Chapter Fifteen

Olivia

"Come on Nims, it's time for dinner." She bounds off the bed and waits for me by the door. I stop to check myself in the mirror. Fancy dress isn't necessary here, but we try to be presentable for the family dinner. Roman won't be here tonight. He is testing some expensive new equipment he had installed. Blair meets me at the top of the stairs, pressing a kiss to my forehead. These men are a dream come true and most days I can't believe my luck. Three men. I didn't even really date when I was younger, and now there are three of them. The truce between them is still fragile, well, fragile in regards to Duncan. He is the only one not entirely ok with everything. And the only one continually pissing me off. Blair is fine with it. Polyamory is the norm in shifter society. Callum took to it rapidly, possibly because he hasn't been the biggest fan of vampire society. And maybe because he and Blair get along so well. Duncan, though, he seems to struggle with some jealousy still. I think Callum doesn't especially help. He has a trickster side to him that enjoys baiting Duncan.

Callum comes from the right and meets us at the base of the stairs. "Ah, you found our girls first. We can all walk to dinner together. Duncan will be overjoyed to see everyone."

Blair snorts and I shake my head at Callum, "Must you provoke him?"

"Until it isn't fun, yes. All he would have to do is stop being bothered. That's it. Honestly, Blair was the first one dating you, if I understand correctly. He is the only one that would have any sort of claim to being annoyed and he isn't. Duncan needs to grow up. I'm helping him."

Blair laughs out loud as Duncan comes from a side hall. Duncan frowns when he sees all of us and Callum says, "Hello Duncan, we were just talking about you."

Duncan rolls his eyes, "Wonderful. Olivia, love, how are you this evening?"

"Better. And hungry. Any idea what's on the menu?"

"No, but it smelled amazing when I walked past the kitchen."

With everyone gathered, we move a little faster to get to the dining room. The moment we are seated Roman's employees bring out dishes. Duncan was right, it smells amazing.

We are all quietly eating when Duncan asks me, "When did you tell Roman about the trip?"

What an odd question. "I told him the next evening at breakfast."

Dunca's face twists a moment before he asks, "When

did you start having breakfast with Roman? He always said he preferred to be alone at the start of the evening."

With a shrug, I tell him, "He invited me sometime before we left on our trip. I had breakfast with him after we got back. I really appreciated being invited."

Callum nods, "I actually was with her when she told him. I thought you had gone with her at least once. What with the way you follow her around."

Blair chimes in, "I've gone with her as well. Roman has been very welcoming when I have been with her."

Duncan looks salty as fuck, saying, "I don't understand why you never mentioned it."

I can't help but laugh. "Oh? The way you mention things to me? Or do you somehow think I should make sure you are aware of every detail of my life without you putting forth any effort? Sir, be for real. You treat information like a commodity. And I am reciprocating that behavior. If you want more transparency, it will start with you."

Duncan glares at me. "You don't know enough about vampire society for me to share everything with you."

"And you certainly had no desire to help change that, did you? No, better to keep me in the dark and let me fumble things. Callum has been teaching me about vampire society since we left here. That didn't change when we came back. He is still teaching me. Blair is teaching me about shifter society. Roman is teaching me how to lead. Ailsa is helping me to learn my magic. And you have the fucking nerve to be mad at me for not sharing my life when all you have done is try to keep me in the dark? Miss me with that. Fuck you Duncan.

I'm taking our dinner and Nims and I are going to eat in my room. If you follow me, Duncan, I swear I will set you on fire. I've had all of you that I will tolerate for the evening."

Nims growls in Duncan's direction when he starts to say something and he shuts his fucking mouth. Good. About time he kept that thing shut. One of Roman's employees comes running in with a cart, pulling up next to Nims and I. They say, "Allow me to assist you, please?"

"You don't have to, we'll be fine, really."

"Ma'am, we want to. Please let us do this. Plus, Marie sent desserts for you and the pup. She would hate for you to miss out on them."

They pull back a curtain on the cart to reveal a large iced dog biscuit in the shape of a bone next to a dish of Cranachan. With the curtain pulled back, I can smell the raspberries and the touch of whiskey, the cream and the honey used to sweeten it. Oh, how could I say no to this? "Well. I can't deny Marie her pleasures and I will certainly enjoy the Cranachan. Give her my thanks and thank you as well. Here, let's get me up to my room before anything else happens."

My plate and Nims' are quickly set on the cart, along with my glass of blooded wine and Nim's bowl of chilled blood. Once the cart is settled, Nims and I lead the way out of the dining room.

Blair

"I think that might be a record for how quickly you've

made her mad. You know, if you don't like her, you should just not date her."

Duncan scowls harder. The fool thinks he is intimidating. "I like her. But she is unlike any other vampire. There is so much she doesn't know. She doesn't respect our ways. I'm trying to help her understand how to move in vampire society."

Callum laughs. I can see the traces of blood on his lips from the blooded wine he was just drinking. "Duncan, I hope Roman never calls upon you to lie. You are bad at it. She understands how to move in vampire society. You know that. What you are missing is that she isn't our equal, nor is she beneath us. She is so far above us that we will spend our lives trying to keep up. I know I relish the challenge. I think Blair does as well." His eyes flick toward me as I nod. Fascinated by where this is going. "I think you also see it as a challenge, but one to be squashed rather than to rise to. And that is why you are going to lose her."

Duncan slams a fist on the table. "I am not losing her. We just don't see eye to eye yet. She'll come around."

A growl erupts from me. "Duncan. You are the one in need of changing, not her. You should tread carefully. I will not tolerate you trying to force her to change to your liking."

Duncan stands, slamming both hands on the table and hissing at me. "Fucking try it, wolf."

As I rise, Callum rises as well, but he reaches out and places a hand on my shoulder. "Blair, she hasn't decided to stop seeing him. It will hurt her if you turn him into wolf kibble."

Gritting my teeth, I say, "Watch it, vampire. You are treading on thin ice."

Duncan retorts, "I'm ready when you are."

Niall runs in, skidding to a stop. "Duncan! What are you thinking? Roman wants to see you, *now*." Duncan snarls and stomps off. Niall turns to us and says, "My apologies. Roman will reprimand him. He knows better."

"That won't stop this. His behavior toward me isn't the problem, it is his insistence on trying to change Olivia. To make her small. That is going to get him killed."

Niall looks grim. "I understand. I will speak with Roman. He won't appreciate the slight to his daughter. He appreciates you standing for her."

Chapter Sixteen

BLAIR

Waking up next to her is the best. I don't get to do it nearly enough. She stretches and snuggles into me, sighing. "It's always so nice to snuggle into your warmth. Temperatures haven't been an issue for me in a long time, but I find that since the demon side of me emerged, I really enjoy heat."

"You can enjoy my heat any time you like."

She giggles, "I'd love to, but Roman is expecting us for breakfast."

"I should tell you, Duncan and I had words last night."

"Oh. Well, I'm not surprised. He seems quite determined to piss everyone off lately."

"Yes. Roman may have some things to say about it. He sent Niall to fetch Duncan. Niall said that Roman would not appreciate the slight to his daughter."

"What did he do after I left that Roman would consider a slight?"

"Nothing that he wasn't trying to do in your presence. He hasn't figured out how to accept you as you are yet. Wants you to change for him."

"Well, that's not happening. I refused to change for my parents. There is no way I will change for him. I meant what I said last night. You and Callum and Roman and Ailsa have all been so supportive. He has made me angry ever since the day I met him." She chuckles. "Which also happened to be the day that I finally said yes to you."

"I thought you knew him before?"

She climbs out of bed, grace and gorgeous. "No, I knew the bartender a little. And this one vampire kept chatting at me every time I went in there, but other than that, I wasn't interacting with anyone. In fact, the guy that had been chatting me up was thrown out because he flew off the handle about me smelling like a wolf."

I know who it was. He is an asshole and tries to intimidate us every time he walks by the store. I might have to step outside next time. See if he recognizes the scent that was on her that day. Maybe he'll decide to fight me about it. "Really? And the other vampires stopped him?"

"Yes, Duncan threw him out while Roman and Ailsa came to talk to me. I didn't know it yet, but I was about to become so much more involved in the vampire world. Now that I know more about the vampire world, I sometimes wonder if I should have run that day."

My body freezes just for a moment, in shock that she still thinks about leaving. The fear that one day she might. Would I ever see her again? "I'm glad you stayed."

She pulls a shirt on and says, "Yeah, me too." She comes

to sit on the edge of the bed. "I've been talking with Roman about making some big waves in the vampire world. It isn't going to be the safest thing I've ever done, but it may be the best thing for the magical community as a whole if the vampire community drags its enormous head out of its own ass."

I can't help but laugh at her description of the vampires. "Oh gods, don't let them hear you say that. They are really stuffy about that sort of thing, and I just know they will take offense."

She shrugs, "As long as I don't need to. But I will do whatever is necessary to protect my Nims. Now, want to come with me while I walk her before we have breakfast with Roman?"

"Of course."

Roman is visibly pleased to see Olivia when she and I walk into his suite of rooms. It is odd to see his face so expressive. In public, his face is a mask and nothing shows. Coming to breakfast with Olivia has revealed a side of him I didn't think existed. After they have finished greeting each other and Nims, Roman acknowledges me. With that over, we seat ourselves and start eating.

Roman asks Olivia, "What are your plans for the day?"

Olivia finishes chewing and says, "I have lessons with Ailsa. I'll be coming directly back home once I finish. We plan to take one of the armored vehicles and they said something about sending out decoys as well, but I don't know for sure."

Roman nods his approval. "I like it. Decoys are a good idea. Blair, will you be traveling with them?"

"Yes, I believe Callum plans to as well. Duncan was planning to. I don't know if his plans are changed after last night?"

Roman grimaces. "Yes. They are changed. Niall will travel with you. Duncan can ride in a decoy vehicle. His behavior last night was poor and my employees were so horrified by it they ran to let me know. Olivia, I am so sorry. I haven't entirely decided what to do with him yet. I would welcome any ideas you might have."

Olivia shakes her head no. "I really don't want to be involved in punishing him. I just want him to see me as a person. I don't think he is a bad person exactly, but his way of thinking... about me specifically, it leaves much to be desired. I don't know if we will continue to see each other."

Roman nods. "If he gives you any grief when you break up with him, you let me know and I will assign him elsewhere. I have more enforcers and I often rotate them out. He'll know why it is happening, but that won't matter. He won't be allowed to victimize you for not staying with him."

Olivia sighs. "I don't think it will come to that. At least, I hope not. I know he is capable of treating people with respect. I've seen him do it. I just don't understand why he doesn't treat me that way."

"Because he's dumb." Roman snickers and Olivia gasps. "Look, I know he isn't unintelligent. But he can be intelligent and dumb at the same time. I know you must've heard someone described as the dumbest smart person? That is Duncan. He's real fucking dumb for being as smart as he is. All he has to do is respect you as a person and you are so easy to respect. You are kind, giving, and intelligent as hell. You are more powerful than any one of us. Possibly more powerful than all of us together. I don't think Duncan even realizes he could push you too far one day and you could immolate him with a thought." Her face drops and I hurry to say, "I'm not talking about by accident. I mean on purpose. Your control has become fabulous since you and Ailsa figured out your powers."

She smiles, only a little watery at the edges. Nims bumps Olivia's shoulder with her nose and she gives her Nims a hug. Roman clears his throat. "Well, I suppose we should all get going about the rest of our evening. I need to give my system one final test run just to check—."

We all hear someone running down the hall like their ass is on fire, the footsteps drawing closer until a quick knock and they burst into Roman's suite. I don't recognize the vampire, but Roman does, and he says, "Yes Wesley, what is happening?"

"We are surrounded. Italian vampires and those hunters, they are converging on the estate."

Roman nods. "I had hoped to have more time. Put the plan into action. Go!"

The man nods and dashes out of the room, leaving the door standing open. Roman looks at us. "It would appear tonight is the night. I'm sorry, but you are going to miss your lessons. Ailsa will be here shortly. You three should go get dressed. Get Callum with you as well." He looks at me. "You and Callum stay by her side, no matter what."

I nod, and he turns, striding off to a different room. Olivia says, "I guess we should go."

Olivia

The house is a hive of activity as I emerge, fully dressed and ready for battle, Nims at my side. Blair and Callum meet me in the hall. As we head for the first floor, a messenger rushes up, telling me I need to meet Roman in his office.

We hurry that way. When I arrive in Roman's office, I see Ailsa. Ailsa asks Blair and Callum to wait outside. She shuts the door behind me, and I see another woman; she's tall, dark, and stunning.

"Olivia," Ailsa says, "I'd like to introduce you to Lilith."

My eyes widen, and Lilith reveals a spectacular set of wings. She studies me, and my wings pop out, unbidden, as do Nim's wings. She smiles broadly. "So, you are one of my grandchildren?"

I nod, saying, "Yes, I believe so. Do you know how we could defeat my father, or at the very least, get him to leave me alone?"

She laughs, telling me, "He is one of mine; defeating him is never easy. I thought he was locked away all this time, stuck in hell where he belonged. Now I find he is out and the head of a cult. I have no idea how many children he has spawned or how many he has spawned and murdered to take their power. For all I know, he has another twenty of you waiting in the wings, so to speak," she says with a wry look at her own wings.

"For now, what you need to know is that not only can you fly and set things on fire, you'll be able to do deep magics that most," she glances at Ailsa, "most cannot do. I will need to teach you the ways of flight, as not all of my grandchildren inherited the wings."

I ask her, "Can you tell me why Nims seems to be sharing abilities with me?"

She notices Nims, possibly for the first time. Her eyes swing back to my face, and she says, "I have an idea, but I am unsure. For now, if you all live through this battle, I will teach you things. But this battle is human things and I cannot interfere."

"But this battle is only happening because of your son. All of these people are here hunting me for him."

Lillith nods. "I understand, nonetheless I cannot interfere. He has not directly set this battle in action. I know my son. He will have many others making the decisions. Even the hunting of you, he will not be directly involved beyond expressing the wish."

"Dammit. Ok. How will I get in touch with you?"

Ailsa says, "I will teach you how to call her. Her grandchildren, even the ones without wings, have their own way of calling her."

My eyes round as I realize what Ailsa is saying. "Then I suppose we have a lot more to discuss than I realized."

Lilith nods. "Yes, two of my grandchildren will have much to discuss. Since they are the only two that have lived beyond finding out they were half demon. Once the battle is done, and you are recovered, Ailsa will help you call me. And I will come and teach you how to fly."

With that, she disappears. I look to Ailsa. "We need to discuss how you haven't mentioned that you're technically my sister."

She nods. "We will, once this battle is finished."

Chapter Seventeen

OLIVIA

We leave the office, with Roman behind us. Callum and Blair come to stand on either side of Nim and me. Roman heads for the stairs to the basement, but before he reaches them, a voice booms throughout the house.

"Send the girl out, and I will let you live."

My eyes are drawn to the window, where I find a sight that freezes my heart in my chest. The man from my nightmares, the man who has spent years hunting me, always with that silver cross sharpened to a point at the end. His eyes are locked on mine. I can't breathe; everything in the house fades into a sharp ringing and his eyes. Suddenly, the sprinklers come on outside, and the man is pelted with white paint. Black lights snap on everywhere, and the man of my nightmares is covered in glow-in-the-dark white paint. Time and reality snap back into place. Our eyes are no longer locked. I hear Callum asking Roman, "Why are the people outside covered in glow-in-the-dark paint?"

Roman shrugs, saying, "We needed a way for the

witches to differentiate between one set of vampires and the other. So I rigged up a sprinkler system that would spray them with glow-in-the-dark paint. At the same time, I had black lights installed throughout the yard. This way, it didn't matter whether it was day or night, there would be clear differentiation."

Blair laughs. "You covered a bunch of vampires and hunters in white glow-in-the-dark paint so the witches would know who to shoot? That is priceless!"

Roman says, "Yes. Now all we need to do is give it about ten minutes to dry."

Callum

Roman shouts orders left and right, sending people to different doors, waiting for the word to attack. He has the front doors opened, and as they open, he shouts out, "If you go away now, we'll let you live." The look on his face shows he has no expectation that they'll leave; he just wants to throw their words back in their faces. The hunters, along with the Italian vampires, laugh as they run forward, attacking those at the front doors.

The signal is given, and the ones waiting at the side doors rush out, flanking them. The shouts and screams are like music to my ears. Olivia begins to try and creep closer to the fighting, Nims moving with her as one. I don't think she even realizes her wings are still out. Even as I think that, her wings and Nim's both disappear. Blair gives me a look, and we both stay right next to her. I nod, my tongue going to that one sharp canine, the small amount of pain and blood centering me in ways that not much else will.

I can see the fighting much closer as we follow Olivia. There's blood and glow-in-the-dark paint everywhere. I'd like to be out there in it, tearing out throats, stabbing people with their own crosses.

I see Roman wade into the fighting. He looks like one of the Highlanders from times long gone. All that's missing is the kilt and sword, perhaps some blue paint.

Olivia takes another step closer. She wants to be in the fight. I look towards Blair, a silent question on my face: Do we stop her, or fight at her side?

Blair answers my question by flexing his muscles and clenching his fists. A thrill of anticipation goes through me. I can see the one that had locked eyes with her. He is fighting, trying to work his way to her. I can't wait to kill him.

Chapter Eighteen

Olivia

Another step. And another. I can't stay out of this fight. Every part of me wants to dive in, especially my demon side. I can't stay away from it; the smell of blood, the violence, it calls to me like the song of a siren. I'm just at the edge of the fray, Nims still at my side. I think she's struggling to hold back, too. I look at Callum and Blair, and I know they won't stop me. Both of them are preparing to wade into battle with me. I think I know now why they're my favorites.

People close in on either side, attacking Callum and Blair. Before I can decide who to help, Sprenger and Kramer are in front of me. Sprenger grabs my left arm; Kramer grabs my right. They lift their crosses, chanting. Horror flows through my body, freezing me. Then Nims attacks Springer. She bites into the arm holding mine, causing him to scream in pain. That scream unlocks my body. I didn't realize my eyes had shut until they flew open. My wings sprout, stabbing Kramer in each shoulder. He screams in pain and fear, swinging wildly with his cross to try and stab me. I block him with one arm, and his cross hits Springer in the face. I turn to check on Nims; she's feasting on Springer's insides. Her wings are out too; she uses one to knock the cross out of Springer's hand as I watch. The other is firmly planted in his back, holding him in place. I turn my attention to Kramer. He spews at me, "You'll die like the demon you are, and when you are dead, we'll harvest your soul. You'll feed our Lord and master, furthering our cause, whether you like it or not. Even if you kill me, more will come for you."

I laugh in his face. Grabbing his shirt up at the collar, I pull him close and whisper in his ear, "You won't live to see what I do. But I get to make you pay for all the time you spent hunting me. You'll never hurt anyone else again." His eyes widen and his jaw goes slack with fear as my teeth lengthen, and I lean forward, sinking my teeth into his flesh. His screams are as delicious as his blood, and I drain every drop of life from his body. Only when there is nothing left do I drop his carcass.

The fight is still going hard and heavy. I wade into the fray, stabbing anybody with white paint on them, using wings and claws, once even my tail. Nims is right there with me. We wreak havoc on their numbers. About halfway through, I spot Diane just a couple of feet away. She sees me at the same time and turns to run. Nims and I are on her before she can get two steps. The wings may not have me flying yet, but they are useful for an extra bit of speed. She screams and flails as I hold on to her. I look down at Nims. "What do you think, sweetie? Should we bring Callum a little present? A little Diane snack?" Nims barks, and that is agreement enough for me.

Diane screams louder, calling for anyone and everyone to help her. It does her no good as I wade through bodies and a few fights still going on, dragging her behind me. As I reach Callum, he kills the person he's fighting with and turns a questioning look on me, saying, "Where have you been? We were supposed to stay close to you. We can't do that if you wander off."

With a smile, I push Diane forward, saying, "I left to get you a present." Diane is shivering and whimpering at this point.

Callum looks up at me and smiles so big. "Father is going to be so pleased." Then he reaches forward and rips Diane's head off her body.

Blair

I watch Olivia as she drags Diane's struggling form over to Callum. Gods, she is magnificent. She looks absolutely feral as she presents Diane to Callum. I watch as the blood splashes on her and Nims when Callum rips Diane's head off.

Her enjoyment at watching that bitch die is shared by Callum and myself. We've both held a grudge against her since she imprisoned Olivia. I look her over, checking for injuries, and I realize she has horns. I wonder if she knows? Watching as she drops Diane's body to the floor, I ask her, "Did you know you have horns?"

She gasps, "What? No way!" She dashes off to a mirror. I can see the disbelief on her face as her hands come up to touch the horns she sees in the mirror. Her face is slightly changed too; it has just a hint of darkness around the edges, angles a little sharper. Her reaction goes from shock to wonder and I think settles on happiness. She doesn't look upset about it, and that's what's important. She turns to Nims and inspects her but finds no horns. Then she tells Nims, "We should put away our wings."

The two of them work to put those away. It seems to take a little longer than usual. I wonder if it is because she still feels a little bloodthirsty. Grinning, I tell her, "You could bring some of that back out later if you like."

She laughs, and then a messenger arrives, stepping over bodies and handing a thick envelope to Roman. A really bad feeling rises up from my gut. I just know that the envelope is nothing good.

Roman opens the letter, reads it, and looks directly at Olivia. "They know."

Olivia kneels and clutches at her Nims. "They can't have her. I won't let them. I'll kill every damn one of them if I have to. We can bath the world in their blood. They won't have my Nims."

Roman nods. "I agree, we're going to fight this. We'll do what we must to ensure her safety."

Olivia looks up. She smiles at Roman. "Maybe it's time for that change in the laws we've been talking about."

Roman grins. "Precisely what I was thinking. I haven't been training you to be a leader for nothing. For now, let's clean up my damn yard."

Chapter Nineteen

OLIVIA

It's been a week since the battle here at Roman's house. During that week, Ailsa spent the majority of it teaching me and revealing some truths.

Ailsa is one of the half-demons born the last time my father was free and walking the Earth. One of an even smaller number that survived. It still feels strange to know that I have a sister, and that she has been training me all this time. I asked her if she knew or suspected when she first met me. She said no, but she felt like she needed to keep me close. She was drawn to me in a way that she had never experienced.

She said that is why she made the decision to buy animal blood from me and to keep a watch over me. She felt like I would be important to her somehow, even if she couldn't quite see how. Once she began to suspect, she couldn't tell me that she thought I was her sister, not until she had more proof.

This week we spent many hours teaching me how to

call Lilith. Now I could call Lilith in my sleep if I wanted. However, I think perhaps she is not someone I want in my dreams. So today, I'm locking myself away in my bedroom, all the men banished for the night. Callum understood, as did Blair. I'm still not talking to Duncan. He isn't happy about that, but I've told Roman that I'm not ready to see him yet. Therefore, Duncan stays away at Roman's order, whether or not he likes it.

Tonight is for calling her. I hope to learn more about my lineage, about my father. I really want to know if all the stories about her are true. Was she really out there killing babies, except for the ones that wore some special charm with certain angel names on it? Or was she feared for other reasons? Are those fears more about her power? No way to find out unless I go ahead and call her here.

Calling her takes seconds, and she appears almost immediately. She smiles. "I knew it wouldn't take you long. It didn't take Ailsa long either. Of course, she had to kill her teacher for the spell, but he really had it coming. He was only withholding it because he knew exactly what she was and wanted to keep her under his thumb. Once she realized it, it was over. He never saw it coming."

I can't help but enjoy the fact that my grandmother is bragging about my sister murdering the man that tried to keep her as his pet. I ask her, "How did we get here? Why did my father go rogue?"

She sighs. "That is a long story. Let us sit and maybe I could pet your dog while I tell you."

"Yes, absolutely," I say. "Nims loves to be petted, and we both love a good story."

We move to the sitting area, and once we're

comfortable, she says, "Perhaps at some point tonight you could tell me how you ended up with a vampire dog when they have been outlawed for centuries." My face must have shown my anxiety. She continues, "Don't worry, I fully approve. The dogs were never the problem. The problem was always the owners. It is still always the owners that are the problem."

"Oh, good. Then the tale is easy. It was an accident. Nims wasn't supposed to be turned, but the blood splashed and since we were lying so close, she ended up getting enough to turn her. We were both pretty close to dying already from a severe beating. Honestly, I would have died without her after I was turned. She was and is my guiding light. Everything I am planning is to keep her safe."

Lilith nods her head in agreement as she pets Nims. She says, "I understand. Sometimes the best guides are also our closest companions. Now, your father. He went rogue because there was a war against me, against my power, my independence. They thought I should be subservient. I should do as they wished, simply because they wished it. Lay under his creation while he poked at me like a pincushion. I was young, and I went along with it for a moment, out of curiosity. When I grew tired of the nonsense, I left. And that is when they waged a war against me, trying to force me to go back and to be less. It didn't work. Many of his warriors died for his cause. When killing them didn't work, I seduced his warriors. You all call them angels. I wasn't intending to give birth to so many babies, but it happened. Then they decided that since waging war against me wasn't working, they would kill my children. After which I took theirs. I took their children, and I hid them away. They still think to this day that I was murdering their children. But no, I kept them and I raised them and I made them my own. Unfortunately, the man they wanted me to serve made a mythos of me and caused generations of his lineage to want and fear me. They made some of the most ridiculous spells to keep me away."

Stunned and amazed at what she has said so far, I ask her, "Are they still around? The descendants of those children you took, are they still?"

She nods. "Yes, they are. But back to your father. He was one of my children that survived. However, the constant attacks took their toll on him. Twisted him. He became more like them. And it was only when he fully became one of them that they stopped hunting him."

"What? He became like them? And that was what made them stop hunting him?"

"Yes. And they doubled their attacks on the rest of my children. The ones that were left, they came home. If they were able. I hid them with the children of theirs that I stole. All of them are still hidden away in a secret place. And now I make you the same offer I made to Ailsa so long ago. You can leave this world and come hide with the rest of my children and grandchildren. You don't have to stay here and be persecuted. Be hunted. You could even bring Nims. Everyone would love her."

Her offer is tempting. So tempting. To have a place I could hide where no one would find me. Where I could be among more family while this family would be safe because I was gone. It sounds like a dream. And that is what I worry about. The dream would end. I don't want to be the reason the dream ends for everyone else. I say, "My father knows I exist; he won't ever stop hunting me. I don't want to be the reason everyone else is revealed. And I have work to do here. I'm going to become the head of the vampire council."

Her grin is wicked as she looks me over. She says, "I fully support that. And you're right, your father will be coming for you. Will you overthrow the council and fight your father at the same time?"

"If that's what needs to be done, then yes. That is exactly what I will do."

She looks proud, and I don't know what to do with that. She says, "If there were any doubts that you are one of mine, this conversation would have erased it. You'll need to master your powers if you want to defeat him. He is strong, but strength is no match for knowledge when it comes to magic. Ahriman has never cared for finesse. Delicate maneuvers are not his forte. He is brute force and command, it's why he was so easy for the church to sway. But he'll have followers. He is charming when he chooses and he collects followers like olives in a net."

Swallowing down a burst of fear, I ask, "What if his followers are smart?"

"Then you'll have to be smarter. I will train you as well, to fill in any gaps in the education you are receiving now. Being fully integrated and having Nims, you are too powerful to allow him to have you. You or Ailsa, who lives as a witch. That cover would not work for you as your parents were his accomplices. The only way that I will be able to interfere is if he comes for you personally. Everything I will teach you can only help with your vampire council."

"It seems like I won't have time for anything but

learning. Between Ailsa's magic lessons, Roman's leadership lessons, and Callum's vampire lessons, I might be able to keep walking Nims once we add yours into the mix."

She laughs and shakes her head. "I won't be visiting you or having you visit me. We'll train in your dreams. No one can spy on us there."

"You can teach me in my dreams? Will I remember them?"

"Of course. It's pointless if you wouldn't remember it. And time moves differently in dreams. You will learn much more in one night of dreaming than in a week of waking."

Olivia

I'm in the garden sitting with my Nims when Duncan finds me. He made noise to ensure I notice him. While I feel annoyed about it, I know it was polite and his way of trying to be courteous. I look over and see he has stopped a few feet away from us. He looks unsure of his welcome. Good. He should be. Because I don't know if he is welcome. "What do you want, Duncan?"

"I'd like to talk."

"I feel like maybe you did enough talking." Sighing, I ask him, "What exactly is it you want to talk about? That will help me decide."

He looks away as he stuffs his hands into his pockets. "I thought—no, hoped, we could talk about us. And how I can make it up to you that I let my fears and… if I'm honest, my prejudices, take over how I treated you."

I feel like my eyes are going to pop out of my head. He is admitting to his behavior? Wants to make it up to me? There has to be a catch. A trick somewhere. No way he changed that fast. "I'll listen. For now. I reserve the right to send you away if you sound like you usually do. I've had a good day so far and I would like to keep the happy feeling."

Nims barks, her agreement loud and uncompromising. Duncan nods and crouches in place, keeping his pristine slacks off the dusty cobblestone path. "I appreciate your willingness to hear me out. I'll try to keep it brief. To start with, I know I fucked up. Over and over until even the sight of me pissed you off. This part is not an excuse, but an explanation. I've been a vampire for a long time. I joined the ranks in the more conventional way, with full knowledge and agreement. I was well aware that I attachments were a dangerous thing in this world. I stepped into it fully prepared to never care again. I was overly familiar with loss and didn't care to allow it to touch my life again. Then you showed up at the bar one day. I was stunned and horrified with my weakness. It soon became apparent that I could no more ignore your presence than I could stop being a vampire." He shifts position as he looks around the garden. "I decided I couldn't ignore your presence, but I could stay away from you. Then Ailsa came to berate Roman about not protecting the vampires in his region, and I was set to protecting you."

Nims snorts and lays down next to me, her interest in his speech gone. Smiling, I stroke her head. She is so perfect and more than anyone else in my life, I love her. She is the one I could not do without. The men, I would miss them if they left. They are candles compared to the bond I have with her. She is my light.

Duncan goes on, "As I was around you more, I found my desire and fear for you growing. In many ways I let the fear take over. All of my decisions were rooted in that fear. I don't want you to think I am telling you this because I think you should do something to fix me. This is mine to fix. I know that. I am working my way through the fear. That is my task. My hope is to be allowed in your life, to have a chance to stop pissing you off with my boorish behavior. Maybe you could eventually like my company again. And more importantly, whatever you decide, I apologize. My behavior was shit and you deserve so much better. I was disrespectful and completely ignored that you are a person, not my possession."

Wow, an apology at the end? One that didn't suck? How interesting. "Duncan, I don't know if I can tolerate you closer than a friendship and right now, even that is a tenuous possibility, at best. I accept your apology. I believe you feel remorse for your behavior. Remorse isn't enough. You will need to show me with changed behavior. And there are no guarantees I will have time to even consider you. I am in the midst of, what was it they called it? Ah, extraordinary times. The times I am living through are so far out of the ordinary and I am racing to keep up with the changes. My Nims life is in jeopardy now. The council knows about her. Keeping her safe is my number one goal. Everything else is second to her. Blair, Callum, Roman, Ailsa, you; everyone is second to her. You have been problematic since we met and felt remorse only when banned from my life. I don't have the desire or the time to train you. So, you may talk to me and be a friend. But that is as far as anything goes now. Will it change in the future? Who knows? For now, I am claiming me and my time for the things that are important to me. If you can't act right, your choices are to take yourself somewhere till you regain control or be banished from my world. There are no third chances."

Nims woofs in agreement and Duncan grins at me. "So you're saying there is a chance?"

Rhiannon Futch is a paranormal romance author and Chaos Coordinator, tarot deck collector, rescue dog mom, and craft enthusiast. She has been published since 2019 and is happily settled into writing vampire smut.

Record screech noise here Until the 2024 election she was happily settled into the one genre. Now she is also writing feminist horror novellas, blending her feminism with a dark nature and an immense well of feminine rage.

Wolfie, She-ra, and Daemon are her fully spoiled doggos who live for outdoor games and treat time. She is a night owl with a deep love of fall and winter and teaches yoga to authors but has never managed a headstand.

She is rarely found out in the world, preferring deep woods in the winter and cool writing spaces during the summer. Rhiannon lives in eastern North Carolina currently, with hopes of returning to the mountains of western North Carolina.

If you would like to see what books are next or sign up for her newsletter, visit rhiannonfutchauthor.com (You get a

free book when you sign up!) You can also use the QR code
(on the next page) to get to my website.

Also by Rhiannon Futch

The Daughter of the Moon series-

Selena Rose, Daughter of the Moon Book 1

Thorns of the Rose, Daughter of the Moon Book 2

Heart of the Rose, Daughter of the Moon Book 3

The Fate's Chronicles series

A Vampire's Fate

A Vampire's Treasure

A Vampire's Dream

A Vampire's Chase

A Vampire's Fight

Fated for Halloween - only available via email signup

The Belancore Witches of North Carolina series

Witchy Ever After

A Witchy New Year

My Witchy Valentine

Sin series

Sin on a Dark Knight

Sin on a Broken Heart

Sin on a Burning Heart

Sin on a Vengeful Heart

The Vampire Kings Series

Mercy of the Vampire King

Shame of the Vampire King

Pursuit of the Vampire King

Prey of the Vampire King

Reign of the Vampire King

Love and Vampires Series

Olivia's Fall

Olivia's Prison

Olivia's Family

Warriors of the Old Gods series

A Dream of Blood

A Dream of Wolves

A Dream of Stone

A Dream of Ravens

A Dream of Bones

Her Violent Silence novella series

Wolf Goddess

Coyote Offerings

Old Wolf Woman

Witches Reclaimed series

Titles TBD